THE ALIEN'S CLUE

GRACE KENSINGTON

1

———

Aubrey felt her legs shaking and black spots were dancing in front of her eyes. She couldn't process what Jonah had just told her. It felt as though her mind had simply rejected what he had said and was forcing it back toward him, stopping it from going completely through her thoughts as if that would somehow stop it from being real. She closed her eyes and squeezed them, wanting to stop the spots and regain control.

"What did you say?" she asked.

She felt Jonah step closer to her.

"This patient file," he said. "It's yours. It has your name on it."

Aubrey drew in a breath, concentrating on how it felt filling her lungs and then streaming out so that she could focus. Fill and release. Again. Fill and release. Again. And again. Finally, she felt as though she could think clearly. Her eyes opened and she looked at Jonah.

"Why do you think that it's mine?" she asked. "I'm not the only Aubrey in the world. It's just someone else who went here a long time ago named Aubrey."

Jonah nodded.

"I know," he said, "but look." He held the file out to her, forcing her to look at the metal cover. "It has your last name. *My* last name. And the middle initial is the same as your maiden name. This is exactly how you write your name."

Aubrey didn't want what he was saying to be true. She didn't want to think that this completely outlandish, unimaginable concept could actually be happening around her. She shook her head again, turning away from him. With Jonah at her back, she couldn't see the patient file. She didn't have to see the look on his face or the concern in his eyes. With him at her back, Aubrey could pretend that nothing had changed. She could imagine a different way that she had met Jonah and a different way that their relationship had grown. She could pretend that there wasn't so much danger and uncertainty laying ahead of them.

"Aubrey," he said, trying to get her attention. When she didn't turn back to him, he continued. "You know as well as I do that just because something doesn't make sense, doesn't mean that it isn't real. I am irrefutable proof of that. If this patient file really is yours, it has to have something to do with this." He paused for a moment and Aubrey could feel the tension that was building in the small, dim space. For the first time, she felt nearly desperate for more light. "I need you to tell me that you have been absolutely honest with me, that there's nothing that you haven't told me or that I need to know."

Aubrey spun around to face him, her arms folded over her chest.

"What are you saying, Jonah? You think that I lived a hundred years ago like you did, but just haven't told you? That I was a lowly member of the crew on the StarCity and that I've been pining for you since then? That you never noticed me when we were hurtling through space or after we smashed into Uoria, but then I found a way to travel to Earth and as soon as I found out that you had come back, I devised a plan to find you and force you to accept me? What is it that you think that I wouldn't have told you?"

Jonah looked remorseful.

"I'm sorry," he said. "I shouldn't have asked. Of course, you've been honest with me. I never should have even let that go through my mind. It's just that..." he lifted the patient file again, "...what if this is yours? How do we explain it? What could it possibly mean?"

Aubrey locked her eyes on the file for a few intense seconds and then lifted them back to Jonah.

"How do we know if it's mine?" she asked.

"We open it," he said. "We read it and see if it has your information in it."

"How?" Aubrey asked. "You yourself said that the patient files are protected from unauthorized access. Each one of them is guarded as part of the 'plague'."

"The purpose of locking the patient files and restricting access to them was to protect the privacy and safety of the patients," Jonah explained. "The computer virus that led to the plague was used specifically to harm people. There was a time when people would use the information that they gleaned from patient files for other fraudulent reasons. They would file insurance claims using another person's identification information, or try to get medications that they could keep for themselves for recreational use or sell. Sometimes they would be able to use the information to steal the financial details for that person and steal their money. That wasn't the case with the plague virus, though.

That was sent out specifically to cause harm to people's health. The terrorists didn't want medical treatment or medications or even money. They wanted to cause destruction and death."

"What does that have to do with why these files aren't locked?" Aubrey asked.

"The files kept by the University medical ward were designed for the ward itself. They couldn't be used for those other purposes because most of that information wasn't even kept in the files, and what was kept there was coded in such a way that only people who worked here would be able to understand it and use it in any way. The locks that were placed on these files were specifically placed there to make sure that the details couldn't be compromised or used to cause harm to the patient. In order for them to be able to harm a patient, though, the patient would have to be alive. A terrorist with the goal of causing illness and pain would have no use for a dead patient."

"So, there was no reason to continue to guard the files once a patient was dead?" Aubrey asked.

"Or at least until that file was no longer needed," Jonah explained. "The locks on the files had to be renewed regularly to ensure that they stayed effective and that the permissions could be adjusted if necessary. This way, if someone did happen to figure out how to access the files, the permissions could be changed and block out threats as well as ensure that no one who wasn't aware of the issue could access the compromised file and use the inaccurate information to attempt to treat the patient. Once the files were no longer necessary, though, they didn't have to renew the locks any longer. If they weren't renewed, the file would go into an emergency locked state for a set period of time and then become inactive, and therefore accessible by anyone who might want to look at them. This made sure that they could still access the information for research purposes or other reasons without putting an actual person's life at risk. If these files were still active, they would have been brought with them when the medical ward shut down and the new hospital was built. They were left here, which means that they weren't needed, or they were being hidden. Either way, they wouldn't have renewed locks."

Aubrey looked at him for a moment and then nodded toward the file.

"Open it," she said.

Jonah hesitated for a moment with his hand flat on the front of the file.

"Are you sure?" he asked. "Once this is open, there's no going back. Once we read what is inside this, we can't pretend that we never did."

"I'm sure," Aubrey said. "The point at which I could have turned back happened before I walked into that lab that day. Once I found you, there was nothing that I could do to change the way that I feel about you, or the fact that I am irrevocably involved in all of this. Even if we didn't read what is inside the file, we couldn't pretend that we didn't find it. It's not like we could just put it back in the file cabinet and act like we never found it and that we are still looking for the same answers that we were before. Because we aren't. Not anymore. There is so much more to this than either one of us thought and if we are going to do it, we have to do it completely and fully. We are already committed to this, whatever it is, and it doesn't matter what is laying ahead of us. We'll face it and conquer it together. We have no choice." She drew in a breath and let her shoulders relax. "Open it."

Jonah mirrored her sigh and nodded. He stepped back

up to the registration desk and placed the file on it. Pulling the lightstick closer so that its full illumination was at its strongest over the file, he tucked his fingers under the metal cover and flipped it open. Just as with his file, the pages inside were made from what looked like slivers of glass nearly as thin as paper. Words appeared on them in text so clear and bold it looked as though it were printed in ink across them, but Jonah knew that they were imprinted into the pages by computer. The pages were crafted in such a way that the only visible text was that which was on the page that was on top at that moment, masking the text from pages below to prevent confusion. When turning the pages, however, the text from all of them became visible again, creating a blur of text that almost made it look as though it was written in a nonsensical language they wouldn't be able to decipher.

Jonah turned to the page of personal details and their eyes scanned over the information on it. Aubrey felt her heart beater harder and more intensely as she saw the correct birthday, weight, height, and other details. Each bit of information that she reached only confirmed that Jonah's initial assumption was correct. This was, in fact, her patient file. Her mind felt as blurred as the words on the pages. She couldn't understand. It just didn't make sense. But as Jonah had pointed out, it didn't matter if this didn't make sense. None of it made sense, and that was exactly why they were trying to figure it out. This was just another piece of this puzzle, another mystery that they were going to have to resolve.

"What is the date on the last entry?" she asked. "If this is actually a file from some time that I was here, then there should be records of each of the appointments that I had.

We should be able to track all of the times that I came here and why."

Jonah nodded.

"You're right," he said.

He flipped the pages to the end and then flipped back a couple of pages. Aubrey could see the look on his face become more confused as he went back and forth a few more times.

"What is it?" she asked.

"There's only three appointments," he said.

"Three?" Aubrey asked, looking down at the file. "There are only three appointments in my whole file? People don't just go to the doctor three times, unless it's a specialist."

Jonah shook his head.

"No. There's no mention of a specialist of any kind. It was just normal appointments. Three times in a row."

"In a row?" Aubrey asked. "What do you mean?"

Jonah pointed at the date at the top of one page, turned it and pointed to the date on the next, and then to the one on the final page of the record.

"These dates show that you came to the office three days in a row." He stared at it for a few moments, the look in his eyes telling her that he was trying to remember something that was just on the edge of his memory. "Look at the year. That's the same year that I left on the Nyx 23 mission. But none of those days make sense. I left almost two weeks later."

"How about any of the rest of the crew?" she asked. "You said that the whole crew had to come in for exams before leaving on the mission and that it was clandestine, so you weren't able to come in at the same time or it would make people suspicious. Could other members have come in that far in advance?"

"I don't know," Jonah said. "We didn't know when the others were going in. I only knew that there were others who were there going at the same time that I did because I saw them when I was here. I was the last person to get my examination. We left really soon after that."

"So, I supposedly went here and saw a doctor, three days in a row almost two weeks before you came for your last examination before you left for Penthos?" Aubrey asked, trying to work her way through the confusing situation and hoping that if she said it enough times, something would occur to her and she would be able to figure it out. "Why, though? What does it say about those appointments? If I wasn't seeing a specialist, there had to be some other reason why they would make three appointments for me in a row. Was it the same doctor?"

Jonah looked at the pages again and shook his head.

"No," he said. "It says here that you saw three different doctors in three different exam rooms." He turned the final page and paused. "Wait," he said, pushing the page all the way open. "Look at this."

He ran his finger down the inside of the spine of the file.

"What is it?" she asked.

Jonah pulled his hand back and looked at his fingertip. There was a red line on it as if something had nearly cut through the skin.

"Glass," he said. "It looks like tiny shards of glass. Like there was another page in the file and someone broke it out."

"I don't understand," Aubrey said. "They broke a page out?"

"Yes," Jonah said. "Like tearing a page out of a book, but these pages are made of glass, so they can act as screens. To get one out of the record would mean having to break it.

But why would someone want to take out a page of your file?"

"It had something on it that they didn't want anyone to see," Aubrey said. "For some reason, that one particular page had something on it that was serious enough that they didn't want anybody to find out about it, even when they decommissioned the record."

"What could possibly be in your medical record that somebody would be that worried about other people finding? Especially when you only came here three times. That doesn't really seem like enough time for you to have done anything that could justify that kind of reaction."

"That's just the thing," Aubrey said. "What if it doesn't have to do with something that I did in the time that I was visiting the medial ward, but the time itself?"

"What do you mean?" Jonah asked.

"These two pages are each for one of the appointments that I had with the doctor. A broken page would mean that the third appointment took up two pages. But that doesn't make sense. What could have happened to me in those two days that suddenly they would need two pages of my file to record everything?"

"But if you came back for a fourth appointment..."

"Exactly. Another appointment, another page. Someone didn't want anyone to know that I came back a fourth time."

"Or maybe what doctor you saw."

"I think that we need to go talk to Nana," Aubrey said. "She says that she and her mother used to look through that book about Nyx 23 all the time. When she gave it to me so that I would find out who you are, she told me that her mother was really focused on the page with your picture. She rubbed it so much that the picture felt rough when I touched it. That has to mean something."

"Did you ever meet your great-grandmother?"

Aubrey shook her head, looking down at her file again so that she didn't have to look at him and let him see the emotions in her eyes.

"No," she said. "She died a long time before I was born."

"Do you know anything about her? What she did for work? Where she went to school?"

"No," Aubrey said.

"What about her name?"

Aubrey shook her head.

"Nana never told me anything about her. I know that it was really hard on her when her mother died and that she never really got over it. When I was younger she would sometimes say that I brought back a lot of memories of her."

Jonah looked at her strangely.

"Brought back memories?" he asked. "That's kind of a strange statement."

"Why?" Aubrey asked.

Jonah shook his head with a slight shrug.

"I'm not sure. It just strikes me as strange. Well, what about your parents? Did they tell you anything about her? Whose child was Nana's, your mother or father?"

Aubrey felt bombarded by the questions, overwhelmed by everything that Jonah was asking. It felt like too much, like he was going too far. Taking a breath, she tried to remind herself that this was her husband, the man who had bared his soul to her and told her everything about himself in an effort only to make her understand how much he loved her. He deserved the same respect and honesty that he showed to her shown to him.

"I don't know very much about my mother and father," she admitted. "I didn't get to spend much time with them."

"That's right," Jonah said as though remembering what

little she had told him about her childhood. "You said that they traveled a lot when you were younger and that you spent the times when they were away and when you were on breaks from school with Nana."

Aubrey nodded.

"I did," she said. "They had always wanted children. At least that's what Nana says. She was my father's mother. She said that from the time that they were just dating they talked about having a big family one day and all of the things that they wanted to do with their future children. They were so excited to build this whole life. But then my mother just didn't get pregnant. They tried and tried, but it just didn't happen for them. So instead they decided to focus on their careers. They both became very successful in their fields. That's why they traveled so much."

"But what about you?" Jonah asked. "Were you a surprise pregnancy?"

"Not exactly," Aubrey said. "It was a few years after they got married and they had pretty much put the idea of having a family behind them. Then Nana went outside her house one morning and literally found a baby lying in a basket on her porch."

"You?" Jonah asked.

Aubrey nodded.

"Me. There was a letter and a few baby things with me, but that's it. She never had any idea who left me lying there. It didn't matter, though. She scooped me right up and brought me inside. She called my parents, who happened to be in town, and they came right over. They decided that I was the baby that they had longed for for so long."

"So, you're adopted," Jonah said, his voice holding an indecipherable combination of surprise and awe. "You hadn't told me that."

"Kind of," she said.

"Kind of?" Jonah asked.

"Well, I mean, yes, I am adopted, but no one knows that. Up until right now only Nana, my parents, and I knew. As soon as they saw me, my parents knew that I was very young. A day or two at the most. My birth mother had literally delivered me and brought me to Nana's house. They decided that they would pretend that my mother had given birth to me at home. They called for a midwife. Nana is extremely well-known in this area and her name gives her considerable influence. She explained to the midwife that my mother had delivered me and was doing absolutely fine, so she didn't need an examination, but that she did need a birth certificate for the new baby. Even though the midwife should have known to examine her anyway, she didn't question what Nana said. She gave them a birth certificate for me and I was officially their child. No one ever had to know the truth. As far as the rest of the world knew, they were just very private about the pregnancy and she delivered a little earlier than expected."

"So, if they were so careful about not telling anybody else what was really going on, why did they tell you?" Jonah asked. "Why didn't they just let you think that you were theirs and never let anyone know?"

"They did for a while. I think that might have even been the plan. But then they realized that even though having a child was what they had wanted so desperately, it wasn't what their lives were about anymore. They loved me. I know for certain that they did. But they figured out that they had put the idea of a family behind them for so long that they couldn't really get back to that space in their minds when they had the opportunity to make those dreams come true. They went back to traveling for work and I started spending even more time with Nana. One day, I was playing in Nana's attic. There were always so many treasures up there. It was amazing. It felt like the whole world was packed into that space. Of course, you know how big Nana's house is, so you can imagine that the attic isn't exactly the size of a normal attic. I didn't know that, though. I just figured that everyone had a space that big to play and explore. One day I was doing just that and I found a basket that I thought was for a doll. I brought it over to a clear spot on the floor where I had been setting up a little house. I tucked my dolly into it and let her play with the baby things that I found with it. When Nana came upstairs a few minutes later, she found me with it."

"Was she angry?"

"No. The opposite, actually. She was happy. Relieved, even. She started telling me a story about a little baby who showed up unexpectedly but was the most wonderful thing in the world and that she had slept in that basket. Of course, I had no idea what she was talking about at the time. She told me that same story over and over when I was little. Every time that I played with my dolls. Finally, one day I asked her if she was talking about me. I don't even know what made me think that. I can't remember any particular thought or event or anything that made it click. It's like she had just said it enough times that it finally sank in and maybe a part of my brain that I couldn't even access remembered it. Does that make sense?" Jonah nodded, and Aubrey continued. "Anyway, that's when I found out. We sat down with my parents that night and talked about it. I was expecting them to be mad at Nana, or even at me, but they weren't. I think by then they had figured out that that wasn't a secret that was theirs to keep. They said that I deserved to know who I was and even though they loved me just as if I was their own child, there was part of my identity that I would never be able to know if they pretended forever that the first couple of days of my life didn't happen. We even started celebrating my birthday twice. Once on the day that they believe that I was born, and once on the day that they adopted me."

"It doesn't sound like you being adopted was ever a problem for you. Why didn't you tell me about it?"

"Just because I'm not embarrassed about it doesn't mean that I really want to tell people. My parents intended people not to know, and I feel like I should respect that. I guess that's silly."

"Do you see your parents often?" Jonah asked.

"No. I haven't seen them in a couple of years. They've been traveling so much, and I've been working. We don't really have much chance to coordinate with each other." Aubrey shook her head, trying to dispel the gloom that had settled over her. "We just need to go talk to Nana. She has to know more about this than she has told me. It can't just be that she sat with her mother and looked at the pictures. She has to have said something to her."

"We should take the rest of these files with us," he said. "Just grab all of them. I don't know if any of the other ones have anything to do with any of this, but if there is any chance that they are here for a reason, then we should have them."

THEY SCOOPED all of the records out of the drawer of the file cabinet and headed out of the medical ward. By the time that they reached Nana's house, the sun was just starting to lighten the horizon, but Jonah wasn't tired. Adrenaline was running through him and he felt like his body was buzzing with the energy that it caused. They carried the files that they found into the house and put them on the kitchen table. He started the coffeemaker to make Aubrey a cup of coffee as he did every morning. She drew in a breath of the rich smell.

"That smells wonderful," she said.

"I figured you're going to need it," he said. "It's almost time for you to leave for work."

Aubrey shook her head as she looked down at the stack of files on the table.

"No. I'm going to take the day off."

"You are?" Jonah asked, feeling shocked. "What about the project in the lab? Won't they need you?"

"I'm sure they will," Aubrey said. "But you need me, too, and you are always going to be more important. Besides," she reached for her file and held it up for him to see. "I'm pretty sure I'm sick."

Jonah gave a short laugh and carried the mug of fresh, hot coffee to the table. He put it down and went to the refrigerator for the cream. The thick white ribbon cut through the blackness and then billowed up from the bottom of the mug, swirling into a smooth light brown. He added a sprinkle of sugar and stirred it before handing the mug over to her. Aubrey took a sip and Jonah watched her shoulders relax as the sweet flavor flowed through her.

"We should bring all of this stuff into the study," Jonah said as it suddenly occurred to him that soon Gannon, Mordecai, and the rest would be waking up and coming down the stairs. "I don't want to get anyone else involved until we absolutely have to."

Aubrey nodded and grabbed a handful of the files. They carried them into the study and rested them in the center of the massive dark wood desk in the center of the room.

"Wait here for Nana," Jonah said. "I'll go upstairs and get the book and the rest of the files."

She nodded again and took another sip of her coffee. Jonah rushed out of the room and up the stairs toward their bedroom, thinking about coffee, doctors, and the busy, thrilling days that led up to him leaving Earth and spiraling into the unknown.

2

____

Tenley folded another of the cloaks over her arms, trying to ignore the feelings that were bubbling up inside her. Before she could get the garment the rest of the way folded, however, her arms dropped, and she turned toward Michael where he stood across the bedroom, emptying the large wardrobe.

"Are you really sure about this?" she asked.

It felt like she had asked the question dozens of times already since Rain first appeared, but she couldn't stop the thought from moving through her mind. Michael seemed so confident, but she couldn't bring herself to feel the same way. She wished that she could. She wished that she could have the same positivity and drive that her husband did. He looked at her and she could see that he was frustrated but was trying not to let that frustration develop into anger toward her. This was challenging for everyone and he was struggling to be sympathetic toward the difficulty she was having even as he felt his own excitement toward the possibilities that were ahead.

"Yes," he said, dropping the clothes in his arms to the

bed. "We've been over this. I've told you that this is exactly what I want. It's what I've been dreaming of for more than 115 years. It's what both of us have been dreaming about."

"Is it?" Tenley asked.

Michael looked at her strangely. He took a step around the bed toward her.

"How many times have we laid right here in this bed talking about Earth? How many times have we thought about what it would have been like if we hadn't been on the crew and didn't end up here?"

"I know," Tenley said, tossing the cloak onto the bed.

She could remember making that cloak. It was one of the first garments that she had made for Michael after they crashed on Uoria. She was ambitious and determined to move forward then. Though she had heard some of the rumblings throughout the crew that they shouldn't give up and should keep trying to find a way that they could return to Earth or at least communicate with mission control, that hadn't been her first compulsion. Instead, she went into survival mode. Her mind blocked out any reality beyond what they were experiencing right at that moment and she immediately pushed ahead to make sure that they would be able to get through that first afternoon, then the night, then the next day. Every moment was an accomplishment and she focused entirely on preserving the strength, morale, and cooperation of the crew. It was all too possible that the entirety of the crew would rebel, small factions within them breaking off and choosing to fight against those who didn't agree with them rather than attempting to cooperate. She strove to prevent that, to keep them united and ensure that whatever they were going to do, they were going to do it together.

As hard as she pushed in those first few hours, days, and

weeks to make sure that the rest of the crew stayed focused and they were able to establish the beginnings of a settlement to keep them safe on the strange and foreign planet, Michael had pushed in the opposite direction. He wanted to immediately try to build a vehicle that would sustain them to the nearest space outpost. Even if they were able to get to a small planet that hadn't yet cooperated with Earth, they would have a chance of utilizing their technology to communicate with mission control and mobilize a rescue unit. She compensated for this pressure with more efforts to settle. He had started pulling apart what was left of the engine of the StarCity in a feeble attempt to restructure a vehicle from the salvaged parts and so she began to pull apart the seats and the carpeting, salvaging the threads and the fibers from them so that she could repurpose them. It took her several long days, but soon she learned to take those threads and weave them into fabric that was soft and warm, ideal for making into cloaks that they could wear to protect them against what they learned was often unpredictable and sometimes bitter weather.

Giving him the cloak was a message. It was meant to tell him not just that she loved him and wanted him to be comfortable, but also that there was more to taking what was left of their mission and giving it new life than trying to get off of Uoria. She wanted to show him that they could have more, that even if they had to stay here for a time, they could turn what they had into what they needed. She never allowed herself to think that they would be there forever.

Then things changed. Time passed. Years went by. Michael abandoned the parts of the engine where they lay and eventually they disappeared, going into some other project and taking on new meaning for the crew. What Tenley had thought was going to be just crisis mode, managing their new reality step by step became daily life and soon thoughts of trying to get off of Uoria had disappeared from her mind. Even when they awoke from the lock imposed on them by the Covra, her goals hadn't changed. She was happy to just go back to the life that they had established for themselves, even letting the arrival of the Denynso roll over her as though nothing different had happened. Then Rain suddenly appeared again. Everything shifted and the fire within Michael was back.

"You always wanted to go back to Earth," Michael said. "You always wanted to leave here and go back to the life that we were supposed to have."

"No, Michael," Tenley said. "That's what you wanted. I talked about being on Earth. I wondered what it would be like if we had never left. I never talked about going back. If I had a choice, I would never have thought about Earth again."

"But why?" Michael asked. "Earth is our home. It's where we built our life."

"No," Tenley said again. "It's not. It's where we had the life that we used to have. It's where we met. But that was only the foundation. That wasn't our life, Michael. This, right here, is our life."

"This is far from anything that we ever knew, Tenley. This isn't a life. When we joined Nyx 23 we were young. Everything was exciting and thrilling. We had no concept of anything that might happen to us. We thought that we were going to be able to save the world and couldn't possibly face any real consequences. Then we ended up here. It took everything from us."

"It didn't take each other," Tenley said. "We might have been together when we were on that ship, but this is where we really fell in love. This is where we really learned about each other and how to rely on each other. This is where we got married and had our first home together. The settlement is what we know. Uoria is our home now. It's been more than 115 years since we left Earth. We don't know anything about that planet now. We don't have a life there or a home. That's all gone. What we have is right here. Each other. The life that we built here. Our home. Our marriage."

Tenley felt her throat tighten with emotion and heard her voice grow high and sharp. She took a breath to calm herself and turned back to the clothing in front of her. Out of the corner of her eye she could see Michael come around the side of the bed toward her. He reached out and took her waist, pulling gently on her until she turned to face him.

"This stopped being an adventure a long time ago, Tenley," he said softly. "This was our dose of reality, forcing us to realize what could really happen."

"I don't think that it's an adventure," she said. "That's not why I want to stay here. I want to stay here because it isn't an adventure. It's comfortable. It's home. I worry that that is why you want to leave."

"What do you mean?"

"I haven't forgotten the type of person you were when I first met you. I remember the spark that was inside of you. There was nothing that could scare you. Nothing that could keep you from taking on a challenge or finding that next thrill. As much as you say that you can't stand being here and that you wish so much that you were back on Earth, I honestly believe that if before we got on the StarCity someone was able to tell you that we weren't going to complete our mission and instead were going to end up on some distant planet that hadn't even been identified yet, you wouldn't have hesitated. You would have thought that was an amazing prospect, something that was even better than just being able to free a prison colony. It's a whole new world! A new experience! Something that no one has ever seen before. You wouldn't have seen the danger or even if you did, you would have thought that that just made it even better. That part of you still exists and I think that it's that part that's making you so excited to leave here. You are craving another adventure. You want something more than what you have here."

"That doesn't mean that I want more than you."

"It might as well."

"What about you?" Michael said, sounding almost angry now. "You used to have that fire in you, too. You were the one who found out about the Nyx 23 project and convinced mission control that we could be trusted to be a part of it. Then we got here, and all of that was gone. You didn't even want to try to get back. You just gave up the second that the StarCity crashed."

"Gave up?" Tenley asked disbelievingly, pulling out of his hands and taking a step back away from him. "Is that what you think I did?"

"What else am I supposed to think? Everyone was scrambling around trying to figure out how to get back on course or how we were going to contact mission control, but not you. You were just resigned to being here and didn't care about whether we ever got away."

"Everyone was scrambling because our ship had just smashed into the ground. People were dead. There was blood and broken glass and twisted metal everywhere. The sky was black with smoke and fires as far as we could see. Don't you remember any of that? Don't you remember how terrifying it was when we realized that the ship's control was gone and that we were just hurtling toward the ground? We didn't know if we were going to survive the next ten minutes much less the next day or week or month. When we had crashed and we made it out of the ship, all that mattered to me was that we were both breathing. I couldn't think about the mission anymore. The mission didn't matter. It was over. It was gone. Our pilot was dead. Our friends were dead. Our ship was destroyed. What did matter was figuring out what we were going to do next. I didn't give up. I kept going. You were thinking about the past and going backwards. I was making sure that we would have a future." She drew in a shaking breath. "Now you want to throw all of that away."

"I don't want to throw anything away," Michael said, some of the softness coming back to his voice. "That's not what I'm doing. I know how hard you worked to make sure that we got the settlement in place and that we all could get back into as normal a life as possible. But I always thought that you wanted to get back to Earth as much as I did."

"There was a time when I did," Tenley admitted. "Once we were settled into life and life seemed like life again, I started thinking about going back to Earth and being able to pursue all of those plans that we talked about, things that we never would have been able to do on Uoria. Then we got married. We found out about the Mikana and life became easier and more comfortable. A few years passed. This became home and I stopped thinking about Earth. The only time that it ever really crossed my mind was when you were talking about it. I knew it was something that you wanted so much and I couldn't bring myself to ask you to stop talking about it. So, I listened to you. I shared your thoughts and your dreams, and I talked about what I thought it might be like if we were there. But I never thought that it would happen. We had already tried everything that we could think of to communicate with Earth or to get off of the planet. Even the Mikana couldn't help us. We didn't know about the Denynso. There was nothing that we could do and I didn't see any point is us continuing to try so hard. It was just wasting the life that we had trying to think of a way to get to a life that we might have had if things had turned out differently."

"And now?"

"It hasn't changed. The thought of going back to Earth doesn't excite me. It doesn't make happy. It terrifies me. What is the planet like now? What will they think or say or do when they find out that we are who we are? We have no idea what the military or the government are like now. Maybe they won't want the public to find out anything about us and what happened to us, and they will take steps to make sure that they never do. Here, we know what to expect. Here, we know where we are and what life is like. Here, we're safe."

"That's just the thing," Michael said. "We aren't. We aren't safe. We don't know what to expect. We didn't know what to expect when the Covra came and we didn't know what to expect when the Denynso came. We didn't know what to expect when Rain came back. Life here isn't any more predictable than life on Earth, it's just smaller. We have a chance to get out of this settlement and back to the mission that we thought we were going on in the first place. You heard what Rain had to say about the war that is on Penthos. What's happening right now has been going on since before we ever left Earth. This is about us just as much as it is about any of the rest. Don't you want justice? Don't you want to make sure that everyone who is responsible for this is held accountable?"

"Us being here is what really brought us together," Tenley said. "If we didn't crash here, I don't know if you ever would have wanted to settle down. You might have never figured out a time when you thought you were ready to stop traveling and create a home together. What happens if we leave? If we go right back to Penthos and to whatever is waiting there, what is going to happen to us? And Penthos—do you really want to go back there? Don't you remember what happened when we were first there? It was horrible. I don't ever want to see that place again. I don't want to remember what I saw there any more clearly than I already do. How could you?"

"Because I have always carried with me the horror that we ran away. We didn't accomplish what we went there to do. When we left Earth it was with the intention of getting to Penthos, finding out as much as we could about the prison colony, and making a show of strength so that we could then mobilize a rescue effort that would free the prisoners and bring the guilty species into custody to be dealt with by the Intergalactic Committee. Instead, we got there and we panicked and then we fled."

"We freed some of the prisoners," Tenley protested.

"Yes, a few. But what good did it really do? Rain has already told us that when the Earth military went back to Penthos there was no sign of anyone there. No one. Not the people running the prison colony. Not the prisoners. No one. Those prisoners obviously didn't get away. I don't know what happened to them, but it seems to me that us getting them out of their chains didn't really do them much good. All we did for them was make them fight for themselves again. Then we abandoned them. We just left them."

"We didn't just leave them. We followed protocol. We weren't equipped to handle an assault to that magnitude. That was always the plan, and you know it. We wanted to go there and make a difference, but we knew that if things started to get too intense and dangerous that we were to get back into our ship and immediately reach out to mission control for reinforcements. We had no way of knowing that the Valdicians were going to sabotage our ship and compromise our communication and control systems. That was something that we couldn't prepare for and that wasn't our fault. We did what we had to do."

"And countless people suffered because of it. You might feel differently, but I can't stand the thought of everything that happened because we left when we did. If we had stood our ground, things might have been different. Mission control would have figured out that we hadn't responded and would have sent exploratory teams or reached out to roaming guard ships and directed them to us for help. We could have kept the Valdicians there rather than letting them get back to Earth and start all of this."

"You don't know that," Tenley said. "The Valdicians were able to convince the humans that did come to create an alliance and begin the experiments. Who's to say that they wouldn't have done that to any of the teams that might have arrived?"

"No one," Michael relented. "But we don't know. The point is that we didn't try then and now we have the chance to make it right. We can't just throw that chance away."

"I don't want to be thrown away either."

"Tenley. I could never do that. I would never just put you aside. Marrying you wasn't something that I did because I had to. It wasn't something that I did because we ended up here and I had no other choice. You're right. I was wild when we were on Earth and the thought of settling down and not traveling wasn't something that I ever contemplated. But that doesn't mean that I thought any less of you. Any time that I thought of the next mission or the next journey, you were always right there with me. That hasn't changed. Me loving you isn't reliant on us being disconnected from the rest of existence or having our lives taken from us in the way that they were. I love you." He stepped up to her again and looked deeply into her eyes. He leaned forward and touched his lips onto each of her eyelids as she closed them. "I love your eyes for everything that they've seen and the way that when they look at me I know exactly what you are thinking and feeling." He kissed either cheek. "I love your face for being the most comforting thing that I saw the entire time that we were on the StarCity and every single day after, and for being what I want to see every morning and every night for the rest of my life." He kissed her lips and she pressed hers against his, seeking the familiarity of his taste. "I love your lips for the sound of your laugh, for every time that you tell me that you love me, and for always being the one to tell me the things that I need to hear." He brushed his lips across each of her earlobes. "I love your ears for listening to me when I need so much just to let everything that is inside me out and for never making me feel as though I should be embarrassed for it."

"Michael..." Tenley breathed, but she felt his fingertip touch her lips.

"Shh," he said. "I'm not done." He touched a kiss to the spot just above her heart and she felt herself shiver with the feeling. "I love your heart for the incredible beauty that is there, and the strength. The courage. The determination. The love." He ran his hands down her arms from her shoulders and intertwined their fingers to lift both hands in front of him so he could kiss the back of each. "I love your arms and your hands for always being there to hold me when I need it, and all of the times that you have been able to manage the work of three people when others around you were giving up." Michael lowered himself to his knees in front of her and gently moved her shirt up and out of the way so that he could access the skin of her stomach. He ran a trail of kissed from her chest bone down the center of her stomach to her navel, where he let the tip of his tongue dip briefly before looking up at her. "I love your body for everything that it has been able to accomplish and everything else that it will do. I love you not because we're hidden away from everything or because of all of the danger and challenges that we've faced, but in spite of it. I will go on loving you no matter what we do. As long as we are together, that's all we need."

3

Rain rose up in her seat and glanced back over her shoulder to check on the progress of the other vehicles. She had only arrived back at the Mikana kingdom a few hours before and had taken just enough time to eat and take a short rest before gathering up people who were willing to help pilot the other vehicles back to the settlement to collect the rest of those who had committed to coming with her back to Penthos. The other vehicles were at a slight distance from her but still close as they moved swiftly across the planet. It was reassuring to see that Athan hadn't fallen out of their formation. Though they hadn't given her enough details to tell her what was really happening, Creia, Ellora, and Kyven had told her enough that she knew that they were in serious danger. Knowing this, she had hesitated to accept Athan's offer to help her bring the rest from the settlement. She didn't want to put him at any higher risk than he already was, but he had convinced her that it was that risk that made him the ideal person to go along with her. The people who were coming after him were the same people who had kept those vehicles hidden before he stole them. They already knew that he was the one who had stolen them. Going with her wouldn't put him at any further risk except putting him out in the open, which he didn't feel was much more of a risk with the other vehicles close to him. Anyone else who was piloting one of the vehicles, however, was also in danger. She had accepted that danger when she first took the vehicle to go to the settlement. He didn't want to pass along the risk to anyone else if he didn't have to.

They were nearing the settlement and Rain felt the bubbling of nerves in her belly. It was all getting so close. Once they had everyone who was willing to go along with them, they would go back to the kingdom and train for their return to Penthos. There had been no turning back for some time now, but there was a tremendous sense of finality in this step of the process. As they approached the settlement and she saw the people milling around in the center street, corralled close to the front of the village by the massive stone wall that bisected the street, she missed Lynx more than ever before. She wished that he could be there with her, helping her through this, but she knew that he was where he needed to be just as much as she made the right decision in coming back to Uoria. She was the only one who would be able to pilot the ship properly and the lives of those who were aboard relied on her to get them to the safety and the medical treatment that they needed, while those on Penthos needed her to gather the supplies and the reinforcements that would strengthen them in their fight.

Their vehicles swept through the gate and came to a stop several yards away from the crowd. They climbed out and headed toward the people closest to them.

"Is everyone ready?" Rain asked.

"There are still some who say that they want to go but

who haven't come down yet," Gideon said. "They shouldn't be long."

"Do you know how many people are coming?" Rain asked. "Will we be able to transfer everyone in these vehicles?"

"Excuse me."

Rain turned around and saw Sara stalking toward her with long, determined strides. She carried a basket on her hip and inside Rain saw a mound of fruit freshly picked from the orchard at the far side of the settlement. Her face was tense and angry, and she seemed to be keeping her focus away from Rain, choosing to look into the distance instead.

"Thank you, Sara," Rain said. "All of the supplies that we can bring with us will be a help."

Sara pulled the basket back toward herself and turned her eyes toward Rain.

"This isn't for you," Sara said, her voice almost sinister in its slow, controlled tone. "This is for my family. I can't imagine that you need much more help than you already have."

Without another word, Sara turned and Rain watched the other woman stomp away from her, heading back to the village.

"Don't let her bother you," Gideon said.

"What's wrong with her?" Rain asked.

"She isn't responding well to those of us who have decided to leave. She isn't the only one."

"Why?" Rain asked. "All of us would have left in a second if we had had the opportunity when we first crashed. It might have been a long time ago, but we have the chance now. What's wrong with taking that chance?"

"Like you said, it's been a long time since we crashed

here. Families have formed here that didn't exist before. Children have been born. A lot of those people are comfortable here and can't imagine their lives if they tried to go back."

"I can understand that," Rain said. "I can get that there are some people who would rather stay here because they've gotten used to it, or they have children that they want to raise where they were born and not confuse them by trying to integrate them into Earth society, but what about the rest of us? What's wrong with us taking advantage of the opportunity that's been given to us? With trying to finish what we started?"

"They feel betrayed," Gideon said. "They feel that we built this all together and that leaving it behind is dishonoring everything that we worked hard to accomplish and that we built, discovered, and experienced here. We've been on this planet far longer than we were on Earth and to them that means that we belong here."

Rain took a step back, wanting to be able to see everyone gathered in front of her better. She scanned the crowd, taking in the faces of the people who had come to her, who were willing to face the danger and uncertainty of Penthos again. Most were etched with the years that they had been there, changed from what she had seen in the halls of the University and in the StarCity as they traveled, but still holding a glimmer of that hope and determination, the drive that they had all felt when they were preparing for this journey. There were a few, though, their numbers small but pronounced in the group, that looked almost impossibly young to her. These were the faces of the first children to be born on Uoria. One was Jason, a boy born to a mother who didn't yet know she was pregnant when she went in for her final examination before the journey to Penthos. Rain could remember the angry, heated argument that his mother had had with the head of the team on Earth. They wanted to rescind her permission to be a part of the Nyx 23 program and not allow her to go on the mission because they felt that it was too risky in that condition. Lauria had refused to accept that. She fought hard against them, insisting that she had been able to pass all of the rigorous tests and exams that had been required just to be a part of the department itself, and then the further ones that enabled you to secure a place on the Nyx 23 team. Even pregnant she had been healthier and stronger than many of the other people, and had proven herself capable of handling what they anticipated would be waiting for them on the journey ahead. They had no way of knowing that rather than being gone only the few weeks that they had planned, she would never have the opportunity to experience her pregnancy on Earth and would bring the first baby into their number months after they built their settlement.

Now Jason was standing in front of her, growing quickly into a man. After the century of being locked by the Covra, he was still only just over 16 years old, a year older than the other three who were dispersed throughout the crowd. She was proud of them for standing up, ready to give of themselves for the cause that brought their parents to the only home that they ever knew, and face the uncertainty of visiting the planet that they had heard about their entire lives but had likely never even hoped that they would be able to see. Despite this, she knew that they were far too young to make that decision for themselves. They didn't understand what they were really facing and the gravity of the choice that they were making by leaving the settlement behind. She knew that she couldn't bring them to Penthos with her and put them in such incredible danger. For now, she would bring them to the kingdom and give them an opportunity to experience something more than just the small village where they were born and raised. She would introduce them to Creia, the warriors, and the rest, and let the Creia and Rey decide what they would do from there. In her heart she hoped that they would stay in the Kingdom while they were on Penthos and then they could return to Uoria and make plans to go to Earth.

"If any of you feel that way, please, go home now. I understand, and I will not blame you for not wanting to do this or not being able to handle the challenge. If you feel like this is a betrayal or that it is something that we shouldn't be doing, please go ahead and leave now. I can tell you that I don't feel that way. We left Earth with an intention. We were determined then, ready to take on whatever challenges we could to make sure that we accomplished that intention. I don't think that there is any reason why we shouldn't continue to pursue those goals. Yes, this is our home, and yes, we worked very hard to survive and thrive here, but that doesn't mean that we are tied here. There is a battle still to fight, and I assure you that I will be standing on the front lines as soon as I can be. Those of you who will stand beside me, come. I will be proud to fight alongside you again. Those of you who want to stay here, stay. Make your decision. We will leave here in an hour."

Without another word, Rain turned and started across the compound. She didn't look over her shoulder to see how the crowd might be shifting and who may have changed their mind about going along with her. In those moments it didn't really matter. Instead, she kept her eyes focused ahead of her, the final thing she felt she needed to do before she left the settlement clear in her mind.

Rain walked until the village was far behind her and a

more peaceful quiet seemed to surround her. Soon she saw the rows of stones that marked the cemetery. The sunlight shimmering down on it took away the gloom and made the space looked hallowed and almost ethereal. She remembered the last time that she had been in the graveyard. It was after the final battle with the Covra, after the Denynso came and freed them from the bonds put on them with the virulent toxin that ensured they didn't move while the eggs developed and grew within their bodies. The vicious creatures thought that they had found the ideal nursery for their young when they found the human settlement. They expected that their eggs would be able to develop and hatch at their leisure, devouring their human hosts when they were born to make them strong and healthy after the century that they had spent growing.

The Denynso and the humans who were with them had changed that. Though the warriors had at first been helpless to do anything for them, not knowing what was wrong with them or what needed to be done to free them, they had been there with them and protected them until the team in the compound was able to give them the idea that eventually woke them. The help had come not a moment too soon. By the time that they realized that it would require a human voice to break the people from their lock and bring them out of the deep sleep that had kept the entire settlement just as it had been for one hundred years, the hatching of the Covra young had already begun. Though most had managed to survive the horror by destroying the eggs within their bodies before they were able to hatch, some had not been so fortunate. Either embedded with too many eggs to overcome, too weak to fight the rabid attack of the young once they hatched, or hidden too far out of view for the Denynso or the other humans to find and help them, these people were lost, reduced to little more than their skeleton and skin.

When the battle with the Covra who returned for their young finally ended and the massive stone wall Loralia created secured in the center of the town as a permanent fixture to remind them of what they had faced and overcome, there was a time of both celebration and mourning. Though they were joyful at being delivered from the bonds of the Covra and having another opportunity for life without the overhanging horror of the Covra, there was also the deep sadness that came from the loss of people they had worked closely with and loved. Rain still remembered the intensity of the funeral fire on her cheeks. It seemed brighter and stronger than any fire that she had ever experienced. The wood seemed to wither away beneath the flames in a matter of seconds as the fire burst upward, sending sparks up into the blackness of the night as if they were to become a part of the galaxy itself.

That night had been the first time since the days following the crash that they had experienced the loss of any member of their crew. After they had mourned those who hadn't survived the crash and interred them here in this section of ground the settlement had grown strong and healthy. None had been lost in the years that they spent on the planet before the Covra came and many had begun to look at the cemetery mainly as a memorial to the dead and to the crash itself. The deaths that happened after the Covra attack had been an unexpected and unwelcome shock of reality in the persistence of life. Opening up the cemetery again and permitting the Denynso to mourn with them, honoring the dead with their own funeral rituals, had been almost surreal. Rain had stood there, watching all of it happen, and wondering if anything would ever be like it was again. That night had been an awakening for her, bringing her out of the complacency of the settlement as much as Lynx's love and the efforts of the Denynso and their allies had brought her out of the sleep of her bonds. It reminded her of what brought her here to this planet.

Now the cemetery was as much a reminder as it had been then. This was the last thing that she needed to do to be fully free of this place and the hold that it had had on her. Whether she ever chose to come back, or if she was ever even able to, standing here in front of the graves, acknowledging the lives, contributions, and loss of each of the individuals that now lay beneath her feet, was the final goodbye that she needed to give to this settlement and to the life that she had led here. If she ever returned, it would be by choice and not because of anything that tied her here. She knew that she would always be devoted to resolving what happened, making sure that they found the answers to all of the questions that had been tormenting them for so long, and ensuring that the people of Earth one day knew for certain what had happened to them. She owed that much to the people to whom she was paying her respects and offering her final goodbye. But she would accomplish that with absolute control over herself, her life, and what she would do each day. This was her release, the claiming of her freedom.

Enough people from the settlement had made the final decision to join her that Rain had worried they wouldn't all fit into the vehicles with the supplies that they chose to bring along with them. While some had packed only small sacks that carried just enough to carry them through a short time away from home, telling Rain that they intended to return to the settlement when the war on Penthos was over, others had taken a different approach. Several had stood ready in the street, their feet surrounded by bags and stacks of belongings, everything that they claimed as their own within the settlement or felt that they would be able to use in the new life that awaited them. It was obvious that these people, mostly couples and single men, had no intention of ever returning to the settlement even when the battle on Penthos was over. They saw this as the same opportunity that Rain did, enabling them to finally escape the planet that had been as much an imprisonment as it was a home. She empathized with how they felt, knowing in her heart that despite what the others might feel, recognizing the forced nature of their time spent on Uoria didn't equal bitterness. Just because they were able to admit that this planet wasn't in their plan for their futures and they still wanted to return to the home that they had always known, even if it would be tremendously changed when they got there, didn't mean that they didn't feel love for what they had built there or that they wouldn't carry fond memories with them for the rest of their lives.

Fitting everyone and their belongings into the vehicles was a challenge, but Rain was determined that they would not take a second trip to bring more out of the settlement. It would waste too much time and risk that some of those who were left behind in this first trip would lose their passion and drive. This would take away not just the people that they greatly needed, but also the chance for those people to follow their compulsions and seek out their return to Earth. They were nearly back to the kingdom when she noticed a figure standing directly in their path. Rain was tempted to simply navigate around him and continue on the short distance to the back of the kingdom, but out of the corner of her eye she saw the vehicle that Athan was piloting begin to slow. She slowed her own vehicle in response and then pulled to a stop beside Athan's vehicle a few yards away from the figure.

"Stay here," she said to the people in the vehicle with her. "Gideon, if anything happens, these are the controls. Close the vehicle and go. Don't try to help me. Just go. Get into the kingdom and find Creia and Rey."

Gideon nodded, and Rain stepped out of the vehicle, taking one of the weapons from the settlement with her. She couldn't see the face of the man who they approached slowly. He wore a mask that made his face grey and smooth as if it were made out of stone. His hands were clasped in front of him and he didn't move until Rain and Athan were standing just feet from him. His head turned very slowly toward Athan and he stared at him through the open black spaces of the mask as though he were expecting something.

"Do you expect a greeting?" Athan asked, his voice sharp and icy. "I am the target of the Order. I will no longer comply with the rituals and traditions."

The man shook his head slowly back and forth.

"Then what?" Rain asked. "Why are you here?"

"The Order sent him," Athan said.

"The Order?" Rain asked.

The name pricked in the back of her mind. It was what Creia and Rey had mentioned when they were trying to explain the tremendous danger to her without giving details. Though she still didn't know what had happened or what this person was or represented, just the appearance of the man standing in front of her in his mask gave her a chill that made her understand that this was indeed as pressing and frightening as she had gathered from what the Kings had been willing to tell her.

"They did," the man said.

Out of the corner of her eye she could see Athan's face tighten at the sound of the man's voice. He obviously recognized it and the sound of it upset him.

"What are you here to do?" Athan asked.

Rain's hand tightened on the weapon that she carried, unsure of what was going to happen. She hoped that Gideon was watching carefully and was prepared to follow her instructions if necessary.

There was a long, still pause and then the man slowly lifted his hands to the back of his head. He released the mask and eased it away, revealing a face that seemed far too young for the tension of the energy that was emanating off of him. She expected to see the same darkness and anger in his eyes that she was feeling, but instead she saw something that looked like sadness accented by fear. He looked at Athan almost pleadingly.

"I was assigned to you," he said. "They sent me for you and for those who accompany you."

"What do they want of me?" Athan asked.

"You are to be brought before the Panel on charges of betrayal, treason, and theft for taking the vehicles and for exposing the Order to outsiders."

"What are their plans?" Athan asked tensely.

Rain felt her hand tighten even harder around the weapon in anticipation of what the man was going to say. Her mind flashed to Lynx as she prayed that saying goodbye the day that she left Penthos was not going to be the last time that she saw him.

"You are to be punished," the man said, his voice falling slightly until it sounded almost powdery. "Severely."

"And the rest?" Athan asked.

"They are to be briefed. If they agree to full secrecy, they may be permitted to live in the close watch of the Order." He took a breath. "Except for her."

Rain felt her heard thud painfully in her chest.

"And her?" Athan asked.

"She is your accomplice," the man said. "She is to be eliminated."

Rain felt her muscles spring to action and lunged toward the man, but before she could reach him, he collapsed to the ground. The young man landed on his hands and knees, his head hanging. The grey mask tumbled from his hand across the sand and landed with the empty black eyes staring up into the sky.

"Malcolm," Athan said, lowering himself to one knee in front of the young man and reaching forward to rest his hand on his back.

Malcolm looked up at him, tears streaming down his cheeks.

"Please forgive me," he said desperately. "Please."

His head dropped again, and Rain could see his shoulders shaking as sobs racked his body. Athan tucked his hand beneath Malcolm's chin and lifted it so that the young man faced him again. His expression looked as though it was painful just to look at Athan, but he had turned his face slightly into Athan's hand as if the man's touch was soothing what was ripping through his soul.

"Malcolm," Athan said again. "You don't need my forgiveness."

"I do," Malcolm said. "I saw you in the tunnels. I know the danger that you have been facing, and I didn't help you."

"You saved me in the tunnels," Athan said. "Don't think that I don't know that. You could have led the Panel directly to me. You could have offered me up to them and enjoyed the rewards that I know they would have given you. You didn't. You distracted them and enabled me to get away. You don't need my forgiveness. You deserve my thanks."

Malcolm lifted his eyes to Athan again and it seemed that his tears were only flowing harder now.

"I don't deserve your thanks," he said. "I was sent here to capture you and to kill you if you resisted."

"Have you done either?" Athan asked.

Malcom shook his head.

"No. I can't. "

"Why?"

"I can't accept what they are saying anymore," Malcolm said. "I can't follow them anymore knowing what they have done and that I don't even know everything that they have caused. I can't be a part of them any longer knowing that is what my loyalty and efforts have supported."

"What can I do for you, Malcolm?" Athan asked.

"I need to know everything. Please. I need to know what I've been doing since I was just a child."

"Do you want to be a part of the Order any longer?" Athan asked.

"No," Malcolm said.

"Can I believe you?"

"Yes," the younger man said, and Rain could see the sincerity glowing through his eyes. "Yes, you can believe me. I don't want to follow them any longer."

"Are you asking to defect?"

"If you will have me, I would be honored to follow you, Athan. I don't know all of what's happening, but what I do know tells me that you are on the side of this that I want to be a part of, and I am willing to give of myself and everything that I have to these efforts."

"You know that this is a final decision," Athan said. "If you make this choice, you cannot go back. Ever. Once you have decided to leave the Order, that is the only option that you have. You commit yourself to whatever you left the Order to pursue, or you die. If you want to leave them, it can't be for me or for Rain or for anyone else who is on this side. If you are going to defect, it must be for yourself and with an open, clear, and honest heart. This has to be for you and with the understanding that while we will stand beside you in anything, you are fully and wholly responsible for this decision and for everything that it leads you to. Do you understand?"

"Yes," Malcolm replied. "I understand."

Rain watched as Athan stood and reached down for the younger man. Malcolm wrapped his hand around Athan's wrist and Athan reciprocated. The older man pulled the younger up off of the ground so that they stood facing each other.

"Then you may join us," Athan said. "But be warned. You are putting yourself on the bad side of the corrupt Order. It will take everything in you and all of the hope that you have inside of you of the truth and the hope that the Order once stood for to get through what lies ahead of us."

"Thank you, Athan," Malcolm said. "I am prepared to face anything that is required of me. I swear my total allegiance and loyalty to you and your faction."

Rain felt a slight smile curve her lips. The Faction. It sounded strong and secure, unifying them into one group ready to stand against their common opponent.

4

———

Jacob reached into the oven and pulled out a gleaming metal sheet then carefully reached down to close the door. He stared at the steaming buns on the sheet as he carried it over to the table as if concentrating on them would prevent them from slipping off as had happened more times than he would have cared to admit. He slid the sheet onto the table, smiling at the accomplishment of not having cast any of the buns onto the floor, and took off the heatproof mitts he wore. He was blowing on the buns, knowing full well that that wasn't going to actually help cool them any faster so that he would be able to eat them, when Phaedra walked into the kitchen. Jacob smiled at her and she stepped up to him to give him a kiss.

"Good morning," he said.

"Good morning. That smells wonderful. What is it?"

Phaedra walked around behind him to one of the cabinets on the wall and took out a mug. She pressed it into a recess on the wall and filled it with coffee. He tilted his head and narrowed his eyes at her.

"Phaedra..." he said.

"It's decaf. I promise. I just need the taste."

Jacob laughed and turned back to the buns. They weren't steaming as much now, and he was tempted to slide the whole sheet into the cooling drawer to take the edge of the heat, but he knew that the sudden change in temperature would ruin the delicate texture of the crust.

"I wouldn't think that coffee was something that you were able to have much of in the last year," Jacob said.

He regretted it as soon as he said it, but Phaedra didn't seem upset. She took a long sip of the coffee and shook her head.

"No," she said. "We weren't allowed it at all. I think that's why I want it so much now. I'm allowed to have it, so I want all of it."

Jacob crossed the room to her and wrapped his arms around her expanding waist.

"You can have anything that you want," he said. "No one can tell you what to do anymore."

He felt a thud against his torso and Phaedra curled slightly, giving a small grunt. Jacob stepped back and watched as she rubbed her belly.

"I don't know," she said. "This little one seems to be pretty good at telling me what to do."

Jacob laughed again and took her by the elbow, guiding her over to the island in the center of the kitchen and up onto one of the stools bolted into place beside it. She perched on the edge and leaned forward onto the island with her elbows, holding the mug with both hands.

"He's just hungry," Jacob said. "Or she wants to judge my cooking. Either way, I've barely seen you eat anything for the last few days."

"I just haven't been feeling like it," Phaedra said. "I don't know if it's just pregnancy symptoms or what."

"Well," Jacob said, walking to the other side of the kitchen to open a cabinet and pull out a plate. He opened a drawer and took out a spatula and a fork, "you have to eat. You need the food and the energy. Both of you do. So, I made you my very favorite dinner. My grandmother taught me how to make it when I was little. She came to live with us right after my grandfather died and after school I would always find her wandering around the kitchen making something or another. She would make us these amazing dinners with recipes that had been passed through the family for generations."

"I remember you talking about her," Phaedra said.

Jacob smiled sadly. He had been so lost in his memories of his grandmother and the time that they spent together in the kitchen that he had forgotten Phaedra knew of her. She had never gotten the chance to meet her, but she had seen pictures of them together and heard his stories about her. Jacob's heart ached when he thought about his grandmother. For his entire childhood and his teen years she had been a fixture in his home, always there even when his parents weren't. She had been unlike any other grandparent that he had ever met. She never seemed weak or frail. When they were cooking together she would often mutter that she just didn't understand why his father hadn't just let her stay in her own house. She would have been fine, she always contested. She didn't need someone there to help her. Jacob always smiled and agreed with her, but he knew that it wasn't quite the truth. As vibrant as Meemaw was, she was also dealing with the lifetime aftermath of breaking both hips and a stroke that had nearly taken her from them several years before. His grandfather had taken care of her as much as she took care of him and Jacob knew that alone she would have been in too much danger.

He thought that Meemaw would always be with them. He just figured that she would be there throughout the rest of her life, at least until he was grown and had children of his own. That was when he would feel secure, ready to move forward in his life on his own without relying so much on her. It wasn't long after he left for college, though, that things changed and Meemaw went to live in an assisted living community nearly two hours from the family home. Jacob hadn't seen her in months when he left for the excavation. Going to visit her was the first plan that he had for when he returned home. His throat tightened as he thought about her and the years that had disappeared in the time that he had been gone.

"She knows how much you loved her," Phaedra said softly, obviously seeing the emotion on his face.

"I don't even know if she's still alive," Jacob said.

"You can find out. Once this is all over, you can go back to Earth and find her. I'm sure she will be thrilled to see you."

"I have no idea what they told her, if anything at all," Jacob said. He still had a sense of bitterness toward his parents for how things worked out with Meemaw, but also for the fact that his mother had so easily believed what the company had told her when he disappeared. "Does she think that I'm wandering around Europe somewhere and haven't gotten in touch with them in five years, or that I just haven't bothered to come see her in that time. I don't really know which would be worse."

"We'll find her," Phaedra said. "This won't last forever.

When the fighting is over, we'll go back to Earth and we'll find her. We'll explain what happened. We'll make sure that she knows that you didn't mean to leave her."

"It won't make up for anything."

"It will. At least she'll know that you thought about her and that you haven't forgotten all that she did for you when you were younger."

Jacob couldn't handle thinking about it any longer. He didn't want to think about his grandmother or any of his family. He had chosen to stay behind on the ship with Phaedra rather than joining the rest of the crew in the fight so that he could take care of her and make sure that she was handling everything well. He needed to focus on that, not anything else that was happening around him or that lay in his past.

Forcing himself to smile through the thoughts and the pain that he was pushing to the edges of his mind until they faded away into nothingness, Jacob stepped back up to the table and used the spatula to distribute two of the buns onto the plate. He carried it over to the Phaedra and put it in front of her.

"I can't believe that I never made these for you when we were dating," he said. "I used to eat as many of these as I possibly could whenever I had the chance."

He started cutting into one of the lofty white buns and saw Phaedra narrow her eyes at him.

"Aren't they just rolls?" she asked.

Jacob shook his head.

"That's what they might look like at first glance," he admitted. "But oh, no. You have been deceived. These are far more than just dinner rolls."

The filling inside the bun finally broke through and he

scooped up a bite onto the fork. The rich smell of the meat, cheese, and spices filled the room and he felt his stomach grumbling with hunger. Jacob brought the fork up to Phaedra's lips and she opened her mouth to take it in. As soon as she closed her lips over the fork, he saw her eyes flutter closed and she groaned.

"Oh, wow," she said. "That's delicious."

"I know," Jacob said, taking a bite for himself. "I could probably eat my weight in these things."

"I think that I could, too," she said, taking the fork out of his hand to take another bite. "You know, I have to admit, I'm pretty impressed that there would be a kitchen like this on a ship."

"Oh," Jacob said, snitching the fork back. "I thought that you were going to say that you were impressed by my cooking mastery."

Phaedra picked the rest of the bun up off of the plate with her fingers and took a bite out of it.

"That, too," she said as she swallowed. "But I wouldn't have expected to see something like this on a ship unless it was one of the luxury residential ships."

"This ship might not have been designed for luxury," Jacob said, "but it is a residential ship. Some of the crews remain on these ships for months at a time. There have been missions that have gone on for more than a year without returning to Earth or staying on any planet for more than a few days at a time. This ship has to be as comfortable and accessible as possible for the people who travel on them. I'm sure that they would get tired of the prepackaged rations after a while."

"I guess they would." Phaedra sighed, looking down at the plate.

Jacob went to the table and got another bun to put on the plate.

"Is something wrong?" he asked.

She shook her head, but didn't look at him for a few seconds. When she did, her face looked strained with concern.

"I was just thinking about the rest of the crew," she said. "It's been a long time since they left. I wasn't expecting it to be like this."

"What were you expecting?" Jacob asked.

Phaedra took the fork and poked at the new bun. She shrugged.

"I don't really know," she said. "I guess I didn't really know what to expect. This all happened so suddenly. I think part of my brain is still getting used to the idea that I'm not stuck in that tube anymore. I'm on a different planet, in a ship with you, and I still think that I'm going to turn a corner or come out of our room and Ryan's just going to be standing there. Sometimes I wake up in the middle of the night and I'm worried that if I open my eyes I'm going to find out that all of this was a dream, that you never actually came for me and that I'm still there in that lab."

She shuddered, and Jacob came around the side of the island to wrap his arm around her. Phaedra curled against him, resting her head on his chest and seeming to relax slightly at the sound of his heartbeat.

"I wish that you weren't afraid," he said. "I wish that there was something that I could do to make you feel better or to help you see that nothing like that is ever going to happen to you again."

"I know," Phaedra said. "I know that you are doing everything you can, and I love you so much for that, and for everything. This is me, this is my mind that is broken."

"It's not broken," Jacob argued. "What you went through is unimaginable. No one can blame you for still being scared or for not being completely over it yet. You might not ever be totally over it. And that's alright. I will be standing here by your side no matter what."

Phaedra leaned back and reached up to run her hand down the side of his face. She paused with her palm tucked around his cheek.

"How are you feeling about all of this?" she asked.

"I'm glad that I stayed here so that I could take care of you and make sure that you are alright, but..." his voice trailed off.

Phaedra tilted her head to get a better look into his eyes.
"But...?"

Jacob sighed.

"When I first went to Earth with Jem, I didn't think any of this had anything to do with me. I had just escaped the stream that I had settled in after going through the portal and I was getting used to living in the kingdom with Galadriel and Vyker. Angela had left to live with Jem on his planet and it seemed like life was going to settle down. It had been so long, it didn't even cross my mind to believe that I would ever go back to Earth. Then I went to visit Angela and she told me that she and Jem were going to go back to his planet to help his people. I knew that meant passing through Earth, but in my mind, that was just a brief stopover. We would bring him to Uoria, I would make sure that Angela was safe, and then I would probably make my way back to the stream that I had started to consider my home."

"Then Rilex found you."

Jacob let out the breath in his lungs and nodded.

"Yes," he said. "I had already encountered him, of

course, but I was surprised when he came to us. He told us everything that had been going on and suddenly we went from heading to Uoria to reconnect Jem with the Denynso to being in the middle of a war. I admit that I was angry at first. This wasn't something that I was supposed to be involved in. I wasn't supposed to be a part of this conflict. It had nothing to do with me. I had barely even heard of the Denynso or Uoria, and I certainly didn't know anything about everything that Ryan was doing. I couldn't understand why Rilex and Angela were so willing to go along with it. Even when we first started learning more about it, I didn't think that it impacted me. The only reason that I was willing to be a part of it at all was to help Jem."

"And now?" Phaedra asked. "What do you feel about it now that we're here?"

"I didn't see any connection between me and the fight, but I wasn't seeing the true situation. I wasn't seeing the larger fight. That's changed. I realize now that this is far more complex than I ever could have imagined, and that what happened to me is related to what has happened to you, to the Denynso, and to the hybrids. It's all linked."

"Hadn't you already realized that?"

"Yes, but not like this. It's becoming more and more clear now. I might have ended up on Earth with Jem and Angela by chance, but I know now that I didn't truly go through that portal by chance. There was a reason behind that just as much as there was a reason behind Ryan capturing you, Nyx 23, and everything else. I should be out there fighting with the rest of them. This isn't just about them. This is about us. This is about you and our future child."

He reached down and rested his hands on her belly. It had grown even in the time that they had spent on the ship, telling Jacob that this baby was already heavily influenced by the species that had been mixed with human to create it. Her pregnancy was progressing far more quickly than a human pregnancy, and he knew that she was already thinking about the birth. Phaedra looked down at his hands and joined them with hers.

"This baby will be here soon," she said. "I wish that I knew more about it. Ryan and the creatures he had helping him never told me anything when they examined me. They kept such careful track of the baby, but would never tell me about anything. That was one of the worst parts about being trapped there. I was lying there being prodded and pulled and scanned, and they were talking about me as if I wasn't even there, like I wasn't even alive. Then I would see them recording all of their notes in my file and I knew that they knew something about the baby, but I could never see the notes. Every day that file was right there next to my tank, but I couldn't get to it. I could never see what was in it or what these people knew about what was happening in my body. I know that everything that I want to know was recorded in there. What blend of species makes up my baby. When exactly I was impregnated. The development of the baby. When they expect the baby to be born. If I could only know those things. If I could have just figured out a way to look into that file."

"I saw some of the records," Jacob said.

"What?" Phaedra asked.

"I found records and I went through them. I read some of the information for one of the women in the program."

"Who?" Phaedra asked, her voice rising and her tone beginning to sound almost frantic. "Which woman?"

Jacob thought back to when he brought the file to Pyra,

but he couldn't remember the woman's name. He shook his head.

"I don't know. I can't remember her name. But what I can tell you is that the records of the pregnancy itself were in code. I couldn't understand most of what was in them. Even if you were able to somehow get your hands on your record when you were there, you probably wouldn't have known what they said. That would have been worse, knowing that the information was right there, literally at your fingertips, and yet you couldn't understand it. It's better that you just weren't able to see it at all."

"What else did you find in the file?"

"What do you mean?"

"You said that the part about the pregnancy was in code, but what about the other stuff? What was it?"

Jacob didn't know if he should tell her. He knew how painful it was to find out about the company deceiving his family to cover up his disappearance, and he didn't want Phaedra to feel that. At the same time, she deserved honesty.

"There were letters that were supposedly between her and members of her family. They were supposed to explain why the woman went missing, but it was obvious that she didn't actually write them. I wouldn't think that anybody in her family would believe them, but unfortunately I know all too well that they probably did."

Phaedra looked down at her belly again and ran her hands along it, tucking them beneath the swell as if trying to cradle the baby within it.

"I can only hope that I am somewhere safer when it's time to bring this baby into the world. I don't want my child born somewhere as horrible as this."

"I wonder if this planet was always like this," Jacob said.

"Maybe it was different once, before the Valdicians built the prison colony here. What could it have been if they had never chosen it? If someone had stopped them before they made it here, or when they first built the colony." He sighed and shook his head. "Sometimes I think about Nyx 23 and how the crew must have felt when they got here and they saw the colony. It was already well-established by that point, which means that they knew that there had been years, *years,* that they had been researching other things, going on other missions, while the prisoners were being tortured here. How did they feel knowing that if they had just questioned the planet earlier or put together their mission sooner, they might have been able to stop it?"

"There's no point in thinking about that," Phaedra said. "We can't do anything about it anymore than they could. All we can think about is now."

Jacob shook his head.

"No," he said. "That's not true. There's plenty more that we can think about."

Jacob reached for her hands and eased Phaedra off of the stool. Keeping one of her hands grasped lovingly in his, he led her out of the kitchen and through the ship toward the observation dome. He had been waiting to show it to her since he had heard Ciyrs talking about it and now he felt that it was the right moment. She needed something to calm the ache in her heart and bring the brightness back within her. As thrilled as he was to have reunited with her and to know that they had finally found the commitment that they should have had all along, there was something that was still missing in Phaedra, something that Ryan had tried to kill but that Jacob refused to accept was gone forever. He knew in his heart that she was still there, that all of her still existed deep within her, guarded and blocked by what she had gone through. He simply needed to be patient with her and the process that she needed to go through to rid herself of the pain, fear, and violation that Ryan had subjected her to and someday he would find her again. For now, he could give her a moment of peace and of beauty. What she had said about the planet being such a horrible place had struck Jacob and was still reverberating through his mind. He knew that she felt like she was still tied to Ryan and the breeding facility when she was on Penthos and that she may never be able to escape it. She needed to see that there was much more than just the hardship that existed in the desert and the devastation that the Valdicians caused first and Ryan and his army continued.

They stepped into the observation dome and Jacob closed the doors behind them. The shields were closed, making the room nearly dark with the exception of the bright green emergency lights that created veins of illumination across the dome. He felt his way across the wall until he found the control panel and pressed the large button in the center. The panels of the shields parted, revealing the scattering of stars above them. Phaedra gasped when she saw it and Jacob felt a smile come to his lips at the accomplishment of his goal. He walked back to the center of the room with her and wrapped his arms around her waist, then drew her hand up into his, beginning to sway her gently in a tender, barely perceptible dance.

"We don't have to just think about now," he said to her. He kissed her on the tip of her nose and smiled wider at her grin. "We can think about what's to come. There aren't as many stars here as we've been able to see from Earth, but that's alright. One day, I will dance with you under the brightest, most beautiful stars that you have ever seen."

"You will?" she asked.

Jacob nodded, turning them gently.

"Absolutely. There is nothing that will keep me from being with you now and every day for the rest of my life."

Their mouths were nearing each other and Jacob could feel the tightness in his belly when the door burst open and the pilot stormed in, his face red and tight with anger.

5

"What do you think you're doing?" Frederick demanded as he stalked into the room.

Phaedra stepped back away from him, her hands coming to her belly to hold it protectively. Jacob positioned himself in front of her, ensuring his body was in between hers and the visibly infuriated man.

"We came in here so that I could show her the stars," Jacob said. "She was feeling nervous about being her on Penthos and I wanted to reassure her, not that I owe you any form of explanation."

Jacob's mood had gone from calm and contented to angry in the instant that the pilot invaded the quiet, private space that he had tried to create with Phaedra. The man stomped toward him, his eyes fiery, and he pointed into Jacob's face.

"Do you have any idea what you've done?" Frederick shouted. "Do you know the danger that you've put this entire ship and everyone on it in by coming in here?"

He backed up and crossed the room in three long

strides, slamming his hand against the button on the wall to close the shields over the observation dome again.

"What are you doing?" Jacob asked.

"I'm closing the shields," Frederick said. "And you are not to open them again. Do I make myself clear?"

"Excuse me?" Jacob said. "I don't believe that I ever gave you any sort of loyalty or told you that I was going to follow any commands."

"I don't care what you think that you've agreed to," Frederick said. "By taking down the shields on the observation dome you removed the defenses of the entire ship. You made the vessel and everyone who is onboard completely vulnerable to anything and anyone who might be waiting outside on this planet. I don't care who you are or what you think that you are doing here, it does not give you the right to put everyone in the ship in danger for your own selfish enjoyment."

"Who do you think you are?" Jacob asked, taking a step toward Frederick. "Who do you think you are coming in here making demands of us? The only person who has been on this ship who has any semblance of leadership over the crew is Pyra, and though I have agreed to assist and serve him, even he does not have dominion over me."

"That might be so, but the stupidity of your actions demonstrates just how much you need a leader with you every moment."

"How dare you?" Phaedra said angrily, stepping out from behind Jacob and approaching Frederick. "How dare you say something like that to him. You have no idea who Jacob is, or what he's done. You have no right to talk to him like that."

"I have the right to talk to him in any way that I please. Like I said, it doesn't matter who he thinks that he is or what he has gone through or done or even why he's here, he needs to get it through his head that everything that he does while he's on this ship, and even when he gets off of it, impacts everyone else around him. He can't just think about himself anymore. He needs to realize, *both* of you need to realize, that this is not a game. This is not just a little stop off on some vacation that the two of you are going on. This is an extremely dangerous situation and you need to think about every action that you take because the bad decisions that you make aren't just going to put you at risk. They are going to put every one of us at risk. Feeling like you are separate from everyone else might make you feel important, but it is dangerous. You need to wrap your mind around the fact that you are a part of something bigger than yourself. Even if you don't want to think that you are, you need to straighten up and think about these refugees and the rest of the crew, both those who remained behind here and those who are out on the planet. What you do affects their safety, which means that you are responsible for every single one of them just as much as every single one of them is responsible for you."

The man's words cut through Jacob, but he was still angry. He felt himself bristle, resisting the demanding force that Frederick was exerting, as if digging his feet into the ground as he was being dragged.

"What gives you the right to tell me what to do? You are not the commander of this crew. You are a pilot who was chosen to bring this ship here to Penthos because we had little time and you were the only person we found who was available. Nothing more. If anyone else had been in that transportation bay that night, they would be the one who would have been asked to pilot. There is nothing about you that makes you important or that gives you power or control over anyone on this ship or anyone who has left it."

"It doesn't matter why I was chosen to pilot this ship. The circumstances that led to me being in this position have no application to the reality of this situation. What matters is that I was chosen to be the pilot of this ship and that means that while Pyra isn't here, I am the leader of this ship and this crew."

"You just said that these people are refugees," Jacob said. "They aren't members of the crew."

"Even refugees need leadership," Frederick said. "Any time that people gather, there is the need for a leader. I understand that all of you know and trust Pyra and that I am someone new and unknown to you, but this ship needs leadership and guidance. As the pilot, I am who falls into that role."

"Just because you were chosen as the pilot when there was no other option for getting our ship here does not mean that you are in any form of control over us. If there was a way for us to get you back to Earth without compromising the ship, we would," Jacob said.

"I have no doubt about that, and that alone illustrates even further why you are in need on my guidance. You seem to have some sort of belief that you would be a better leader than me. What is your background?"

Jacob bristled and he straightened, lifting his chin and squaring his shoulders.

"Anthropological research and excavation," he said, then reconsidered the response. "With five years of specialized survivalist training."

"Being able to dig up bones and make up stories about them hardly qualifies you," Frederick said. "As for your survivalist training, as you call it, unless it was administered by the military, it has no merit. I have an extensive military background including training in emergency maneuvers and clandestine missions. I have survived experiences that make this look like one of the pleasure cruises that many of the people I have seen on this ship seem far more suited toward than any sort of wartime efforts. Above anyone here, I am the one who has the experience, the training, and the knowledge to protect this ship and everyone on it, granting you decide to put down self-congratulatory righteousness and agree to do as I say."

Jacob and Phaedra exchanged glances. He could see in her eyes that she was just as wary of all of this as he was. He didn't know what to make of Frederick and his sudden determination to lead the ship. In the time that they had spent sitting on the surface of Penthos, waiting for the rest of the crew to return or to somehow learn of the next planned maneuvers, Frederick had stayed to himself. He had interacted with them only in the most minimal ways, choosing to eat alone and spend the majority of his time in his own pod away from everyone else. Even as those who were wounded began to heal and made their way out into the rest of the ship for short periods of time, the pilot resisted the gatherings. Jacob had assumed that the gravity of the situation was settling in for him and he didn't fully know how to process what was going on. He knew that they had offered Frederick very few details about the situation and could only imagine that he was confused and possibly even frightened by what was happening. Now, however, he seemed militant, driven as if a part of the mission from the very beginning.

"Why are you suddenly called to protect us?" Jacob asked. "What's changed that has made you feel that you need to step in and herd us like your own little flock?"

Frederick stared at him, his eyes burning like embers deep in his face. He said nothing, but Jacob felt like the silence was cutting through him, digging into him more than anything that the man could have said. Remaining silent, the pilot turned on his heel and walked out of the room. Jacob turned to Phaedra again.

"I don't know what to think about that," she said, still staring at the door.

Jacob shook his head.

"Neither do I. Do you think that there could be some ulterior motive? Something that's influencing him that we don't know about?"

"What do you mean?" Phaedra asked.

"This is a man who had no idea what was going on when we came into the transportation bay and asked him to be the pilot for the ship. He has nothing to do with what's happening. No stakes in it at all."

"That we know of."

"Exactly. We thought that we were just picking out a random person who happened to be in the transportation bay and can pilot, but what if that isn't actually the case? We didn't even question why he was in the bay to begin with that morning. He was just there. No explanation. What if he actually was there for a reason?"

"And us asking him to pilot the ship was exactly in line with that reason."

Jacob nodded.

"I think that we need to talk to some of the rest of the crew," he said. "If he does have something to do with this, they need to know too."

They headed out of the observation dome and moved quickly toward the lounges. The first two were empty, but when they reached the one where Bannack and Loralia held their wedding ceremony, they found several of the women sitting at a table that had been replaced in the middle of the room. The small group turned to look at them as they hurried inside.

"Is everything alright, Jacob?" Samira asked, standing up as they approached. "Did something happen? Did you hear from Pyra and the rest of the crew?"

Her voice was frantic and Jacob felt a flicker of guilt for coming into the room so quickly without any greeting or explanation.

"We're alright," Jacob said. "We just need to talk to you about something."

Samira nodded and gestured toward two chairs. Jacob and Phaedra walked to the chairs and he pulled one out so that she could sit down.

"How are you feeling?" Valerie asked Phaedra.

Phaedra nodded, looking slightly surprised but pleased at the woman asking about her. She ran her hands over her belly and then patted it gently.

"Doing fine," she said. "The baby's been really active today. I wish I knew whether that meant that I might go into labor soon."

Valerie shook her head.

"Oh, no," she said. "You've still got some time on you. You're still carrying far too high to be delivering any time soon. Besides, once the baby is ready to be born, there won't be enough room in there for it to be too active. You might feel a few little wiggles and the occasional kick, but if you're still feeling that little one jumping around that much, you still have a ways to go."

Jacob saw Phaedra smile and look down at her belly as if giving her approval to the child within.

"Well, I am perfectly happy to keep it there for as long as it wants to be," she said. "I'd much rather not deliver here on the ship."

Though it was the same sentiment that she had expressed to Jacob in the kitchen, this time the words held the hint of a laugh and he felt a sense of relief that she was feeling more secure and had the support of the other women.

"What did you want to talk to us about?" Samira asked, bringing the attention away from Phaedra and the baby and back to the reason that they had come into the lounge.

Jacob and Phaedra exchanged glances and Jacob took a breath. He explained what had happened with Frederick in the observation dome and the concerns that he and Phaedra had. When he finished, he sat silently, looking at the women and waiting for their response. Samira seemed to be thinking through what he had told them and processing what she thought about it.

"You heard what happened on Uoria with Ullie," she said, not a question, but a statement.

"Briefly," Jacob said, remembering the story that he had heard when they were still in the basement.

"What happened on Uoria?" Phaedra asked.

"There was a Denynso warrior who went rogue," Samira said. "His name was Ullie. There was a war with a species called the Klimnu and in the midst of it we found out that Ullie was cooperating with a human woman to aid the Klimnu and infiltrate the Denynso."

"Who was the human woman?" Phaedra asked. "Was it someone who was part of the exchange program?"

"No," Samira said. "She was a flight attendant who was on the shuttle bringing people from Earth there. We still don't know how she got in touch with Ullie or what she said to him to convince him to do what he did."

"What happened to her?" Phaedra asked.

Her voice was tremulous and Jacob knew that she was afraid of what she might be told. Samira shook her head.

"That's something that Creia, the King of the Denynso compound, handled. The rest of us weren't a part of it."

"Do you think that this could be a situation like that?" Jacob asked. "The way that Frederick was acting seemed so suspicious to me. He has no involvement with any of us, but then suddenly all he seems to care about is leading us and 'protecting' us?"

"It does seem odd," Samira admitted. "It wasn't that he was mean or standoffish or anything," she contended. "It's just that he didn't seem to really want to know what was happening or get involved at all. It's like he figured he would just hide out and this would all eventually be over and he could just go right on back to whatever he was doing when we found him."

"That's another thing," Jacob said. "What was he doing?"

"He was in the transportation bay," Samira said. "He must have been working."

"But on what? Don't you think that if he was getting ready for a mission of some kind, or even just preparing for a cruise or a research field trip, that he would have mentioned it? That he might have hesitated at least a little before agreeing to just leave without any idea of where he was going or how long he might be gone? Do you really think that someone would just walk away from their job and put their entire career at risk just to help someone he's never met, of a species that he's never seen?" Phaedra asked.

"He might have," Jacob said. "We don't know how much Pyra told him. Frederick said that he has military experience. If Pyra gave him the right details, he might have felt like it was his duty as a soldier to help. But even if that's the case, you're right. He probably would have mentioned another job that he was supposed to be doing, or would have tried to make other arrangements before we left. Instead, he just came. Then he sank away. He didn't have anything to do with us until today when he lost it over us putting down the shields."

"How did he know that the shields all over the ship went down?" Valerie asked. "Unless he was in the room with you and saw that you put down the shields over the observation dome, how would he know that the ship's defenses were down?"

It was something that Jacob hadn't thought about, but now the thought only worked to increase his suspicion about the pilot. He was starting to respond when he noticed Leia staring at him.

"What is it?" she asked.

Leia looked at him and shook her head as if she didn't want to say anything, but then tilted her head.

"It's just---" she hesitated like she wasn't sure that she had put the words together properly in her mind. "What do we really know about him?"

"Nothing, that's the point," Jacob said.

"Exactly," Leia said, "but probably not for the reason that you think. None of us knew anything about any of the other ones when we met. If we had relied entirely on assumptions, we wouldn't have gotten this far. We never would have come together the way that we have and there would be many families that never would have formed. Samira, you know. You were there on the Denynso compound and then again in the Mikana kingdom and the human settlement. You saw what happened between Pyra and the Mikana men. He didn't know anything about them and made assumptions that made him dangerous. I under-stand that the way that Frederick was acting seems strange and that all of us might be more prone to being suspicious and questioning anyone new who we encounter. But you don't know what he's gone through or what he's experienced that might have made him act that way. Each of us has our own struggles in our past and our own challenges that we have to try to deal with every day. I'm sure that every one of us would seem strange in some way to someone else if they encountered us in certain situations. I know what it's like to be on a ship that is hijacked. What I went through when I was on my way to Uoria was nothing short of horrific and there are times when I can still feel it affecting me. I know that I'm safe. I know that Gyyx will take care of me always, even when he's not here on this ship with me, I still know that I'm safe because he will do anything that he can to guard me and prevent anything like that from ever happening to me again. Despite that, though, there are still moments when I can feel that same fear that I did when I was on that ship. I can still remember what it was like when I was in the prison before Elianna rescued me. Those are things that are never going to leave me and that I know will impact how I look at the world for the rest of my life."

"Leia's right," Phaedra said.

Jacob was surprised by her sudden contribution to the conversation and looked at her with widened eyes.

"She is?" he asked.

Phaedra looked at him with an indecipherable expression and nodded.

"Of course, she is," she said. "Not a single one of you know what it's like to go through the things that I have, and I don't know what it's like for any of you. I don't know what it was like for you to disappear during your excavation and spend five years in a place that you didn't know and where you could barely survive. I don't know what it was like for

Samira to travel from Earth to be a part of an exchange program on a planet that she had never visited and barely knew anything about, and then to find herself a part of a war for the safety of a mate that she never would have met if she hadn't taken that step. I don't know what it was like for Leia to experience the horror that she did in that prison. But at the same time, the things that I have gone through have made it so that I can empathize with each of you, and I would hope that you would be able to empathize with me. We don't know what Frederick's gone through and how that might still be affecting him. We owe it to him to try to understand him rather than immediately thinking the worst of him. We don't know what he is doing here other than helping us, and we should try to remember and appreciate that."

"But that doesn't mean that we should just put down our guard and not think about the possibility that there is something more going on," Jacob said. "That could put us all in even more danger."

"Of course, it doesn't," Phaedra said. "We have to continue to protect ourselves in every way that we can, and that includes staying vigilant and paying close attention to him and everything that he does. We can't forget, though, that no matter what the circumstances behind it, he is a part of our crew, an important part of our crew, and we should do what we can to respect him as much as we respect each other."

Jacob nodded. He understood what the women were saying, as much as his mind was trying to resist it. All of them came into this battle differently and with their own perspective. Though he was dedicated to doing anything that it took to protect Phaedra and their child, and defend the group that he was slowly beginning to trust and consider his own, he also knew that he couldn't simply reject Frederick or assume that he was doing something that might hurt them. It would do more harm to the group and to the mission for him to keep suspicion locked within him and let it control and distract him from what he needed to be doing both for his family and the rest of those fighting on Penthos and beyond.

"Until Pyra, Maxim, and the rest of the crew come back for us or send word that we should join them, we agree to keep our eye on Frederick, but also to accept that he may actually be trying to help us."

6

———

Samira sat back in her chair and looked at the women gathered in the room with her. They all seemed to be staring at different points in the mid-distance, each lost in their own thoughts.

"Do any of you think that we made the wrong decision?" she finally asked.

They turned toward her and her mother looked at her curiously.

"What decision?" she asked.

"Staying here," Samira said. "On the ship. Do you think that we should have gone with Pyra and the rest of them? Eden went and she has the baby that she is taking care of. Elianna went. Why did we decide to stay here rather than going with the men?"

"Did you really want to face the battle that is happening out there?" Valerie asked. "You know what they said about this planet and about the army that they are fighting. Would you want to see that and be a part of it, or would you rather be safe in this ship, knowing that when the time is right, you'll be able to go out and do your part?"

"The men went and faced the army," Samira said. "The other women went. They are fighting alongside their mates while we sit here and wait."

"You know that Ty would want you to be as safe as possible. He is dealing with enough fighting the hybrids. He wouldn't want to also have to worry about you and want to keep you safe. Doing that would only distract him from what he is supposed to be doing and could put him in serious danger. When you're here, you're safe. He knows that you are protected inside the ship and that when the battle is over and it's safe enough for you to come out, he can come get you."

Samira looked at her mother for a long moment, stunned at what she was saying. This was the woman who had just shown greater courage and bravery than Samira could ever imagine just by reclaiming her life and walking away from a man who had tormented and tortured her for years. She had been confident and strong for the first time in as long as Samira could remember, and even excited at the prospect of the new journey that awaited both of them. Now she was so willing to just sit around the ship, not knowing what was happening to the rest of the crew or seeming to even care what happened as long as she could remain within the ship and not have to face it.

"There are moments when I wish that I had gone along with them," Leia said. "I stayed here because, like Valerie said, I know that Gyyx would worry about me if I was out there with him and I didn't want to keep him from doing anything that he needed to do. I also remember all too clearly what it was like to be in that prison on Uoria and feel every second like I was only a matter of breaths from death, and I don't put it past Ryan or the Valdicians to do the same thing or something even worse to those they get their hands on. But ever since they left, I've been thinking about them and whether we should have been there with them. I know that we could have been a distraction if we were there with them during the battle and they were trying to protect us, but what about when the battle was over?"

"What do you mean?" Samira asked.

"Fighting isn't the only thing that they came here to do," Leia said. "If it was, they would have been back by now. Fighting a battle doesn't take this long."

"Unless they were defeated," Valerie said nervously.

Leia shook her head.

"No," she said adamantly. "If they had been defeated, we would know. The army would have found us here and would have tried to take over. The rest of the crew has not been defeated. But how are they doing? They've been out there for such a long time without us hearing any word of them. Was anyone wounded? Do they have the supplies that they need? Are they safe? Is there anything that we could have done to help them after the battle? Even if we weren't able to actually help them in the battle, we could have been there to help them after."

Samira let out a sigh of exasperation and dropped her hands to the top of the table in front of her.

"This is exactly like it was when we were on Earth," she said. "Staying in that house while the rest were in the laboratory confronting Ryan. All we did was sit there and wait while we could have been doing something that was useful for them. Why did we do that again? Why are we just sitting here not doing anything, not helping?"

"We are helping," Valerie said. "You have to remember that there is more to be done on this ship than just sit here and think about the men and what we could be doing there. There are still wounded hybrids and pregnant women who are here that aren't able to take care of themselves and who need our help. What we are all doing here is so much more than just fighting against Ryan and the hybrid army. We also want to do what we can to fix the damage that he's done and try to make sure that those he has harmed will be able to move forward in a life that is the best that it can possibly be for them."

"I don't understand," Samira said. "You told me that you were happy to be on the ship and out here away from Earth."

"I am, Samira," Valerie said, "but that doesn't mean that I need to throw myself into every conflict that we find. Sometimes stepping back and doing what seems like the smallest things in a situation is the most impact that you can make."

"I just know that I hate the feeling of being so confused," Jane said. "I don't know how we are supposed to handle this situation. We all have our reasons for staying here on the ship rather than going with the men, but now I wonder if they are suffering because we aren't there to help them. I feel completely trapped here. Especially now that this pilot is trying to take over and control everything that we do."

"We agreed that we weren't going to judge him since we don't know him," Samira said, trying to calm her dear friend and reassure her.

Jane looked at her incredulously.

"Seriously, Samira?" she asked. "Are you seriously going to go along with that? When you came back to Earth, all I had in mind was your wedding. I thought that we would finally get to have this big celebration that we had been planning our whole lives and then you would go off and have your life. Instead, I fell in love with a man from a species that I barely knew existed and ended up on a ship on a war planet praying every second that that man hasn't been killed. Right now is not the moment that I want to be scolded for judging someone."

Jane stood up sharply and started out of the room. Samira took a few steps to follow her, but she turned to look at her.

"Not now, Samira. I just really need to be alone."

Samira stopped and watched as Jane continued out of the lounge. She returned to the table and sat down, feeling deflated. Leia stood silently and walked out of the room, slowly followed by the others until Samira and Valerie were the only ones left in the lounge. She turned to her mother and let out a long breath.

"I'm sorry, Honey," Valerie said. "I shouldn't have said anything."

Samira shook her head.

"No, it's alright. I know that you didn't mean anything by it. You were just trying to help. I just wish that Jane hadn't gotten involved in all of this. I feel horrible."

"She has Simran now," Valerie said. "She chose to come with him. She didn't have to. She could have stayed on Earth. She could have decided that all of this was too much and sent him on his way. But she didn't. She decided that he was worth the danger and the challenge that she is facing now. She's angry and frustrated and probably a little bit scared, but she is also doing exactly what she thinks that she should be and what she believes in her heart is the right thing to do."

"She's never been someone who I thought would do anything like this."

"And I am?"

Samira looked at her mother and laughed.

"No," she admitted. "I guess not."

"I guess everyone is full of surprises," Valerie said.

Samira smiled slightly, but then felt the smile melt from her lips as she thought about what her mother had told her the last time that they sat alone together. She leaned forward toward her, hesitating slightly even though she knew that she wanted to ask the question that had been waiting in her mouth since that conversation.

Valerie stood and crossed toward the drink station against one wall.

"Mom..." she started.

Valerie glanced over her shoulder at Samira as she filled a glass. She reached for another and filled it as well.

"Hmmm?"

"There's something that I wanted to talk to you about."

Valerie settled back down in her chair and placed one of the glasses in front of Samira.

"Go ahead."

Samira took a sip of the sweet, clear drink, giving herself a few more moments to think through what she was going to say.

"Will you tell me more about my father? About Martin?"

Valerie's face paled slightly and Samira immediately felt bad for asking. She didn't want to hurt her mother or put her through any more than she was already going through, but at the same time she was desperate to know more about the father she had never known. Ever since Valerie had started to talk about him, she had found herself wondering more about him. There were things about her that she had always felt were so different from her mother and had wondered how they were a part of her. Now that she knew how her parents met and fell in love, she knew that they were a true and tangible link to Martin, the man that was so far different from the stepfather who had been such a source of pain throughout her life.

"What do you want to know?" Valerie asked.

"I don't know," Samira said. "Anything. I've just been thinking about him. Now that Randall is out of the picture, I feel like we're…"

"Free," Valerie said.

Samira nodded.

"Yes."

Valerie took a sip of her drink and sat back in her chair.

"Martin was the most incredible man I ever knew," she said. "He was unlike anyone I had ever met and from the very beginning I just couldn't get enough of him. He made me see the world in a different way, see myself in a different way. I was never a person to think of myself as being smart, or even having the capacity to learn any of the complicated concepts that other people talked about. Your father changed that. He had a way of being able to explain things to me so that I was able to understand them. They didn't seem so frightening anymore, and even though I never caught on to them, or even cared about them, as much as he did, just having him talk to me about things made me realize that I am much smarter than other people would give me credit for in my life."

"You talked about science a lot?" Samira asked, the thought of her father having the same passion for her field that she did warmed her heart and sparked her love for what she knew and wanted to know even more.

"Science, yes," Valerie said, nodding. "He loved science so much. It thrilled him. Every time that he figured something out or learned something new, every time that he found out that I didn't know something and was able to introduce me to it, he got so excited as if he just couldn't wait to share it with me. But that wasn't all that we talked about. We did everything together. We went on trips, we visited museums, we saw historic sites and art. My whole world opened up because of him." She smiled at her daughter and shook her head slightly. "You are so much like him. It's like getting to see a part of him again. There were times during my marriage to Randall when seeing that little glimmer of your father was the only thing that kept me going. It was the most painful thing in the world, because I knew that he never would have wanted me to experience what Randall put me through and would have hated all of the pain, embarrassment, and shame that we both suffered, but at the same time it was the only thing that reminded me that there was something in life that was worth living. Martin had made me feel special and strong and capable of doing anything that I could possibly want to do. He gave me you. I owed it to him to make sure that you kept going, that you knew that there was something more than just life in that house. I don't know if I did a good job of that."

"Of course, you did," Samira said. "If you didn't, I wouldn't be here right now. If you hadn't made sure that I thought that I could handle school and go through it at the speed that I did, I never would have tried. If you hadn't made sure that I knew that I could make decisions for myself and go to live with Zuri rather than dealing with Randall, even if you never said it, I never would have and I might not have survived. If you hadn't made sure that I knew that I was strong enough to handle challenges and that I should follow what was in my heart, even if you did it by never following your own heart, I never would have gone to Uoria with Zuri and Ero, and I never would have met Ty. All of this is because you kept me going, even when you didn't think that you were."

"I know that your father would be so incredibly proud of you. He already was. You were such a dream for him and I have never seen a person as happy as the day that he saw you for the first time."

"Did he hold me?" Samira asked.

"Of course, he did," Valerie answered. "He held you every minute that he could. There were times when I would find him sneaking over to your bassinet and picking you up while you were sleeping just so that he could cuddle with you for a little longer that day." She laughed softly, and Samira saw a veil of tears form over her eyes. "I used to get so upset with him. I just knew that he was going to wake you up and that you'd be up for the rest of the night crying."

"Did I?"

"You know," Valerie said, "you didn't. I can only remember one time when him picking you up woke you up. You had already had a really hard day. You had croup and had been coughing all night the night before and then all day. Nothing that the doctors had told us to try would work and you were just so miserable and tired. You had finally fallen asleep and then he came home from the lab. He had been working late for a few days and said that he had been missing both of us a lot that day. We ate dinner and I went to take a shower and when I got out, he had gone in and was picking you up. I asked him not to, but he did and you immediately started crying. I thought that I was going to absolutely fall apart. But your father was so amazing. He didn't complain or even look upset for a second, even though I knew that he was exhausted too. He held you and bounced you and talked to you."

"What was he saying?"

"I don't know. He kept his face close to you and whispered. It was like he was telling you secrets that were meant just for you. Whatever it was that he was saying, it calmed you down. He told me to go on to bed and get some sleep. He had already asked for the next day off because he wanted to spend some time with us and so he could stay up with you. I was so grateful. As I was heading into the bedroom to get in bed, I heard him singing to you. I woke up a couple hours later, and he was still singing. I don't know how long he walked with you that night, but when I woke up in the morning, he was lying on the couch with you on his chest, sleeping so peacefully. That was the only time that he ever disturbed you, but I think that he made up for it."

Samira laughed.

"I guess so. I wish I knew what he was singing to me."

"I know," Valerie said. "I wish I did, too. I wish I could remember every word that he ever said or that I had something that I could show you, so you could see his face or hear his voice."

"You don't have any recordings? Any pictures? Anything?"

Valerie shook her head, her expression pained again.

"No," she said. "Everything that I had was destroyed."

Samira felt herself stiffen and her jaw tighten with anger.

"Randall?" she asked.

"I had a storage unit that had everything in it from my marriage to your father. Pictures. Recordings. Documents. Gifts. Everything. I knew that Randall wouldn't allow me to have them in the house, but I didn't want anything to happen to them. When things were bad, I would go there and just spend some time looking at everything. I would talk to Martin and pretend that he was there with me. It might sound silly, but it made me feel better. Like I was somehow closer to him."

"That's not silly," Samira said. "It's not silly at all."

"I don't know how Randall found out about it," Valerie said, drawing in a breath and straightening as if trying to withdraw from the memory. "He followed me there one day and found me looking through it. He was so angry. It was terrifying. I remember being so glad that I had brought you to a babysitter before I went to the unit. I didn't usually do that. Usually I brought you with me and I would tell you stories about your father. At that time, part of me still believed that I could raise you knowing him. I wanted to be able to tell you about him and make sure that you knew who he was and how much he loved you. I never for a second wanted you to think that Randall was your father. That was something that I just wouldn't compromise on."

"What did he do when he found the storage unit?" Samira asked.

"He pulled everything out of it and loaded it up in the back of his truck, then forced me in. He brought me out into a field behind one of the farms where he sometimes worked, dumped everything out, and burned it all. It was one of the most horrifying things I have ever seen. There was nothing that I could do about it. I couldn't even cry because I knew that that would just make it worse. Standing there watching it was like going through your father's death all over again."

Samira swallowed the emotion in her throat.

"Did you ever get to go to his grave?" she asked.

"He never got a grave," Valerie said, her voice strained. "I didn't get his body back after his death."

Samira felt her heart drop into her stomach and her vision blurred slightly.

"You never got his body back?" Samira asked. "Like Aegeus? They thought that he was dead when he disappeared from the battlefield and didn't have a body to bury. If you didn't get to see his body and were never able to bury him, how do you know that he's dead?"

It was a hopeful feeling, a lift in her heart that for a moment made her think that there was a possibility that all of the suffering her mother had gone through had been in vain, but that she had the chance that she would one day have the love of her life back, and that Samira would be able to look into the eyes of the father who she had missed even though she didn't remember him. There was no hope in Valerie's expression, however, and Samira quickly knew that her hope had been misguided.

"I know, Samira. It wasn't a mystery when he died."

"How did he die?" she asked.

She wasn't sure that she wanted to know, but at the same time she craved any knowledge about him that she could have. The more that she heard about him, the closer and more connected to him she felt, and she wanted to know everything about him, from how he came into her mother's life, to how he was taken out of both of theirs.

"He died in a car accident on the way home from work one day," she said. "He was so tired. He had been working so hard and not taking care of himself like he should have been. The investigators said that he probably fell asleep behind the wheel and lost control of the car. The car ran into the back of a truck that was carrying hazardous materials. It exploded nearly on impact. That's why I wasn't able to have his body back. It was incinerated beyond collection. All that was left of the car was a warped, melted metal frame. The only reason that they knew it was him was that the force of the impact dislodged the license plate from his car and it flew far enough away from the crash that it wasn't melted. They used that to confirm that it was his vehicle.

That was the only identification that they had, but it was enough."

"I can't imagine not even having a grave that you could go to," Samira said.

"It was really hard at first," Valerie agreed. "I considered having a grave for him anyway, but I didn't want to go through the motions of having a funeral and burying an empty casket. It seemed almost disrespectful, as if it was my grief that mattered in the situation rather than the end of his life. I struggled with that for the first few months, but then it changed."

"You met Randall."

Valerie nodded, looking resigned to the reality that she had created for herself, but also still experiencing the lingering hurt that came from it.

"The tighter that Randall's hold over me became, the more I realized that even if Martin had been able to have a proper grave, I never would have been able to visit it. He would have just laid there with no one to acknowledge him or caring for his grave. I couldn't stand that thought. Once I realized that, it was comforting to know that there wasn't a grave. It was almost reassuring that there hadn't been a body to bury. Not having a body to bury or a grave to visit meant that when I wasn't able to go there to visit him, I wasn't neglecting him. I could carry him in my heart and know that he was there, safe and protected, and that even Randall couldn't get to him or take him away from me there."

"Do you still feel that way?" Samira asked.

Valerie sighed and looked away for a moment before meeting her eyes again.

"I do," she said. "It's been so many years, but even now, I haven't forgotten your father or what he meant to me. Other than you, he was the most wonderful thing that I ever had in my life. Everything that I went through with Randall made it harder to remember that. I'll admit that there was a time when I felt like he had been able to do the exact thing that I said that he wouldn't and had taken the memory of Martin's love out of my heart. It was like he had gutted me completely. I still had my thoughts of him and could see him when I looked at you, but I had lost the vibrancy that he had given me. Then you rescued me."

"I didn't rescue you," Samira said. "You did that for yourself."

"No," Valerie said. "If it hadn't been for you and Ero, I never would have survived. I wouldn't have made it out and I wouldn't be here. I will never be able to thank you for that enough. You didn't just save me from Randall, you gave me back what he had taken from me and reassured me that he hadn't been able to take everything. I'm still what Martin helped me to become, what he saw in me, and I still have him in my heart. You've helped me find that again."

"Why don't I have my father's last name?" Samira asked. "I know that you wanted to remember him and that you wanted to honor him. So why did you make me carry another name?"

"I never had your father's name." Valerie admitted. "When we got married, I kept my last name. It was something that was really important to me then, but I regret it so much now. At the time I felt like keeping my name and passing it along to you was a way to carry on my family's legacy. Martin wasn't close to his family. I never even heard him talk about them. So, it didn't seem to matter to him if their history was carried on. I don't have any siblings, but I was very close to my parents and my grandparents. I wanted to give that to you. I wanted you to be a part of the family that I had had when I was a child, even if you never had the opportunity to know them. I feel so guilty about that now. I realize that just because Martin himself wasn't the legacy of a family that meant much to him doesn't mean that he didn't deserve to have a legacy of his own. You should have been his legacy, a part of him to linger on and carry his name further than he was able to. I should have honored him by giving you his name. Even if it meant changing your name after he died so that you could have that link to him, I should have done it. Maybe that would have made the hard times with Randall more bearable if at least you had his name to hold on to as a reminder of who you really are."

"But the same could be said for you," Samira said. "If you didn't take Martin's name, why did you take Randall's? Wouldn't it have been easier for you to not feel so tied to him? If you had kept your own name the way that you did when you married Martin, maybe you wouldn't have felt so controlled by him."

"Maybe you're right," Valerie said. "Taking his name was something that I barely even thought about when we were engaged. Like I said, I was never in love with him. Being engaged to Martin and planning our wedding was such an incredibly joyful time and I couldn't wait to experience it. I wanted every moment of it to be perfect. I don't even remember Randall asking me to marry him. It was like all of a sudden we were talking about it and then we were standing in front of the judge."

"You didn't have a wedding?" Samira asked.

"No," Valerie said. "It wasn't something that Randall was interested in, and I didn't care. I wasn't excited like I was with Martin. It didn't feel like the joyful beginning that it did then. It felt almost like an ending. They assumed that I was going to take his name and we were ushered through all of the paperwork. I didn't question it or try to resist. I think even then I knew that Randall would have been angry if I hadn't. Maybe part of me even thought that if I took his name, it would somehow make me feel closer to him, like it would improve our marriage if I felt like I had that connection to him. In the end, it just made me feel like he owned me." She took another sip of her drink and stared at the table with the same downcast look that Samira had hated seeing in her as she grew up. "I'm sorry that I wasn't more open with you. I always made sure that you knew that Randall was your stepfather, but I'm sorry that I didn't make sure that you knew who your father really was."

"I still don't," Samira pointed out. "I know his name, but that's it. I want to know more about him."

"Everything that I had of his and that was about him was destroyed, but when we get home, we can research together. We can try to find records and anything else that we can, so you can learn more about him."

Samira smiled through the tight feeling in her chest as she realized that "home" was never going to be what they thought of it again.

7

Eden settled Lysander into the makeshift cradle that they had created for him against one wall of the room that she and Pyra had chosen and gently settled a blanket over him. He was sleeping so calmly and peacefully, blissfully oblivious to the chaos and danger that was happening around him. She hoped that that was the way that it would always be, that he would never be aware of the risks that he was facing and all that he had gone through when he was still so young. In the same breath, she knew that as he got older, they would tell him. They would make sure that he knew what he was born into and the strength and courage he had before he even knew. Just as Loralia had told her when she was pregnant, her son was a warrior, as strong and brave as his father.

Leaning forward to touch a soft kiss to her tiny son's forehead, Eden patted his belly gently and then crossed the room to the bed where Pyra sat. It had been built out of salvaged wood and blankets from throughout the compound, but while it didn't look as comfortable as the bed that they had shared in the Denynso compound on

Uoria, it was better than what they had had in the basement of the lab and Eden felt even more exhausted just looking at it. Her body ached with the exertion of the last few days. Though there hadn't been any fighting, she felt like she had been moving constantly, working to go through the compound and find everything that they could that might be useful, build supplies, prepare food, and help those who were still working to recover from their wounds.

Pyra was sitting on the edge of the bed, one of his boots sitting on the floor in front of him and his hands paused on the ties of the other. He stared down at them, his expression unchanging. She settled onto the bed next to him and took off her shoes, then stood to start undressing for bed.

"What's on your mind?" she asked as she slipped out of her shirt.

Pyra glanced up at her and she saw the involuntary hint of a smile that came to his lips every time that he saw her undressed. It gave her the same boost that it always did, making her feel treasured and beautiful in a way that she had never experienced before she came to Earth. It was so different than the way that Ryan had looked at her. Now that they were here, ready to confront him for everything that he had done, the thought made her skin crawl even more. Where Pyra looked at her with love, respect, and adoration, Ryan had looked at her with lasciviousness, clearly not caring who she was or what she thought or felt.

"It's just really hitting me how much all of this has grown," he said.

Eden sat back on the bed and looked at him questioningly.

"All of what?" she asked.

Pyra straightened and gestured around him as if trying

to encompass everything in the room and the entirety of the compound.

"All of this," he repeated. "This whole situation. All that we've faced and done." He looked at her with a mirthless laugh. "I bet you never would have imagined that giving into Ryan's demands to go to Uoria would have been the beginning of something like this."

Eden shook her head.

"No. I don't think that this rests with me," she protested. "All of this was already happening well before I ever agreed to get on that shuttle and go to Uoria. It would have unfolded just the same whether I had gone or not."

"How?" Pyra asked. "It was you coming and telling Creia about Ryan's plan for you to steal my blood that made us aware of what was going on here."

"But that wasn't the start of it," Eden said. "And it wasn't what actually got the Denynso involved in it. Yes, me showing up in Uoria and talking to Creia made him aware that Ryan had designs on Denynso DNA and was a threat, but the only real result of that was that I was given permission to stay on the compound. Even if I hadn't come or if Creia had sent me away the second that I arrived, the Denynso still would have been at war with the Klimnu. You still would have fought in Loralia's realm and Jem would have still disappeared. The compound would still have gone into mourning for him and the warriors would still have left the compound to explore the rest of Uoria. That means that you still would have found the settlement with the Nyx 23 crew and everything would have happened from there."

Pyra looked at her incredulously.

"That's not how it would have worked," he argued. "The only reason that we were able to find the underground realm was because of you women. We couldn't get through the tunnel, so we wouldn't have found our way down there, which means that we wouldn't have been able to fight the Klimnu down there and Jem never would have disappeared."

Eden shook her head.

"I had nothing to do with that," she said. "That was the other women, the women who came to Uoria with the exchange program. I wasn't a part of that. Even if I didn't come, they still would have and they still would have been able to help you with the tunnel. They still would have gone down there and found the mirrored realm, you still would have gone through the entrances in the orchard, and you still would have had the final showdown with the Klimnu there. It all would have just kept going exactly like it did without me."

"Even if that's true," Pyra said. "Even if we did still have the same battle with the Klimnu and Jem still disappeared, and we still went into mourning. If all that happened in exactly the same way, it still wouldn't have been the same. We wouldn't have been able to figure out how to unlock the Nyx 23 crew if it wasn't for the necklace that Jem made for you and the gifts that the other human women made for their mates, and if it wasn't for the two of us being together, I don't know if those women would have been so willing to bond with the warriors."

"I don't think that's true," Eden said. "I know how powerful the lure of a warrior is. I think that they would have fallen in love in just the same way and you still would have been able to figure out how to unlock them. "

"Well, that only means that we still would have been together, which would have still brought us right here."

"What do you mean?"

"Like you said, we still would have had the other

humans with us and would have unlocked the Nyx 23 crew. They would have then told us what happened to them and we would have eventually figured out about Ryan's experiments."

"How?"

"We would know that there was something strange going on with the crew and then Ryan still would have sent the Valdicians to capture Creia to lure us to Earth. We still would have been there for the wedding because Samira and Ty would still be together, and we all would have ended up in the laboratory. I believe that if you hadn't agreed with Ryan's commands and gone to Uoria, that he would have kidnapped you and put you into the program, which means that you would have been in the laboratory, and we would have been together."

"But the only reason that we ended up in the laboratory was that the Valdicians kidnapped Lysander at the wedding and Jane had that picture, which let me figure out that they were in the lab. If it wasn't for me, none of you would know what to look for or where to go."

Eden was getting confused. They seemed to have reversed their positions on how they saw the situation and now she didn't know what she thought or believed.

"I don't think that matters," Pyra said. "Yes, that's how it worked out, but I don't think that that's the only way that it could have. Even if you didn't go to Uoria when Ryan wanted you to, all of us would still have end up on Earth and nothing would have kept me from you. You are my passion, my love, my everything. You have been intended for me from the moment of my birth and just as I knew that you were meant to be my mate as soon as you stepped off of that shuttle, I would have known that I was going to meet you when I was on my way to Earth and then would have been able to find you. It would have been my draw to you and my need to be with you that would have led me to you and the rest of the crew to the laboratory. We would have found you and rescued you, and we would still be right here, fighting to make sure that Ryan doesn't get away with what he's done and isn't able to hurt anyone else."

She looked into Pyra's eyes and saw the rich orange glow of his eyes, knowing that hers reflected the same color. She reached over and ran her fingers down the side of his face.

"I know that there is one thing that would be very different if I hadn't come to Uoria when Ryan sent me."

"What's that?" Pyra asked, tilting his face into her touch.

"If I hadn't come, I wouldn't have been attacked by the Klimnu. I wouldn't have had to go to the clinic and Ciyrs wouldn't have had to heal me."

"And that would mean that you wouldn't be a Denynso," Pyra said.

Eden shook her head sadly.

"I wouldn't. I would still just be human. I wouldn't be Denynso and I wouldn't be a healer."

Pyra took both of her hands in his and kissed her palms.

"You have done so much good with these hands," she said. "You have removed pain, healed injuries, and saved lives. You are the most amazing thing, the most amazing person, I have ever encountered. There is no other being like you in the entire universe."

"What about Elianna?" Eden asked. "She is a human woman and she gained healing powers when she went to live in the Denynso compound."

Pyra shook his head and drew her closer to him so that he could wrap his arms tightly around her waist.

"It's not the same," he said. "She is still human. She gained healing powers because of Ciyrs, not because of herself. You are Denynso. Your DNA changed, and you are as much a healer as he is. I know that you don't think about that much and that you don't consider yourself like him, but you are. You are talented and skilled, and are invaluable to our kind. But that isn't what matters to me about you."

"It's not?" Eden asked.

She knew that it didn't matter much to Pyra that she had taken on the healing powers of Ciyrs when he healed her back from the brink of death, but she wanted to hear him tell her. She needed to hear the affirmation, the validation of his adoring voice.

"No," he said. "What matters to me is that you are you. There is nothing like looking into your eyes and seeing the rich, beautiful orange that tells me that you are my mate and that you love me as much as I love you. None of the other warriors who fell in love with women outside of our kind have that. They had to wait for their mates to tell them how they felt and no matter what they will always have to wonder what they are thinking or how they are feeling. I will never have to do that. I can simply look at you and know that just as passionate as I am about you, you are about me. You have the same devotion, the same commitment to me. There is nothing more important to me than that."

Eden felt her heart soar, but just before she could begin to respond to him, she heard Lysander coo from his cradle across the room. She turned to look at him and saw their tiny son shifting slightly, sighing as he settled deeper into the bed that they had made for him. His lips turned up briefly in a smile and then his face relaxed as he fell deeper into sleep.

"I suppose there are two things that would be very different if I hadn't followed Ryan's commands and gone to

Uoria when he told me to," she said. "If I hadn't come then and met you, Lysander never would have been born."

Pyra stood from the bed and walked over to the cradle. He crouched down beside it so that he could gaze down into Lysander's sweet face.

"He still would have been born," Pyra said tenderly, the gentle tone in his voice so far removed from the harsh, violent anger that so often defined the Denynso and that had been her first impression of this tremendous warrior. "It might not have been at the same time, but he is permanent. He is irreversible. No matter what, we would have found each other, and Lysander would have been born. He was destined to be here."

Eden climbed off of the bed and joined her mate beside their child. She looked down at him, feeling the same breath of awe fill her that always did when she just took the time to look at him and realize that this amazing little crea-ture, this beautiful tiny baby, was her son. She had never been a woman who had spent much time thinking about being a mother or wishing that she had a child, yet now that she had Lysander in her life, she couldn't imagine a single moment not being a mother, not having him to love and care for and raise to be the best man, the best warrior, that he could be.

"He was," she said, reaching into the bed to run one fingertip along his little pink knuckles. "He was meant to be here and he will do amazing things for his people and for the world."

8

Elianna heard the familiar sound before she stepped into the infirmary. The long, distinct sound of fabric tearing cut through the quiet that had settled around the compound as most of the people there had broken off from the small groups that they had formed during the day and dispersed into the houses, storage buildings, and temporary camps that they had set up throughout the compound to rest for the night. She stepped into one of the rooms that they had set up to treat the wounded and found Ciyrs standing alone in the center of the room, tearing sheets into long bandages that he placed on the table beside him. They tangled around each other, creating a mound that got larger and more chaotic the more strips he added to it.

Ciyrs didn't seem to notice her presence as Elianna came into the room and crossed to him.

"Hi," she said.

He looked over his shoulder at her and finished tearing the piece in his hand into three more bandages.

"Hi," he said.

"Have you been here all day?" she asked.

Even though they had been in the compound together since leaving the ship, she felt like she had had little time to actually spend with her mate. They had both been so busy after battle trying to heal those who had been wounded and assist the entire crew in getting assimilated to their new surroundings in the compound. Though they had all hoped, though silently, that they would spend little time in the compound and would be back on the ship on their way home to Uoria within a matter of days, it had become very clear that that was not the case. They had already been there for far longer than Elianna would have expected them to be, and every day that passed without another battle left her feeling more unsure of the future that lay ahead of them. Though the thought of fighting was frightening and she didn't want to see her mate go back out into the danger, without the fighting there could be no resolution. Something needed to happen, they needed to keep progressing, yet everything seemed to have stalled.

"There's been a lot to do," Ciyrs said. "Some of the injuries are more extensive than I expected them to be and the hybrids are more difficult to heal because of the confusion of their DNA."

"I know," Elianna said. "I know how hard you've been working."

"I feel like I've been tearing bandages for hours."

"You probably have been."

Elianna reached for another piece of sheet so that she could help him tear it into the long bandages that they would use to protect and support the wounds of those injured during the battle, and those still dealing with the injuries that they had experienced on Earth. They tore the bandages for a few silent seconds, the sound of the fabric ripping becoming almost meditative as they created the strips and let the pile continue to build.

"Quimm's healing finally took," Ciyrs said, breaking the quiet.

Elianna smiled at him.

"It did? That's wonderful. I knew that you could do it."

"I was really concerned. It didn't seem like it was that bad of an injury when it happened. I thought that it would just take a session or two and some of the ointments, but he didn't respond. I was scared that we were going to lose him."

"I know you were. But we didn't. He's mending. He'll be completely well soon enough and probably stronger than ever."

"What would we have done if he died?" Ciyrs asked. "What would we do if any of us didn't make it while we were here? I can't bear the thought of leaving anyone behind here. Not even people who we just found on Earth. Even the hybrids who have joined us. None of them, none of us, deserve to be left behind here."

"And no one will be," Elianna reassured him. "The worst for all of them is over now. Their injuries are healing and the risk is less. And when the fighting starts again, we will all be better prepared to handle whatever they have for us."

"And I will be ready to handle the injuries," Ciyrs said. "It's the most important thing that I can do."

Elianna put down the fabric that she held and stepped up in front of her mate. She placed her hands on either side of his face and tilted it so that he looked at her. Leaning forward to kiss him, she offered a warm smile.

"I am so proud of you," she said, the relief in her heart making her feel even more that everything was alright and that the worst truly was over.

"Of what?" Ciyrs asked. "I am a healer. That is what I was born and destined to do."

"Exactly," Elianna said. "The fact that you know that now, that you aren't questioning it or your abilities anymore, makes me so happy. I hated to see what you went through after the baby's mother died. It was like there was a part of you that was missing and without it, you didn't know who you were. I didn't know who you were. Like you said, healing is what you were meant to do. It is wonderful seeing you doing what you were meant to do again and healing those who need it."

Ciyrs brushed a lock of her hair away from her face and tucked it behind her ear.

"Do you know how absolutely incredible you are?" he asked.

Elianna tilted her head at him, looking at him questioningly.

"What do you mean?" she asked.

"You are so supportive of me and encourage everything that I do without even for a second stopping to think that I'm not the one that is actually anything special. Being a healer is what I was supposed to do from the moment that I was born. It is my destiny. I've been training for it since I was young, even more than I have trained to fight. Healing people is as natural to me as breathing and just as expected. You, though, you are something beyond comprehension."

"Because I can heal?" Elianna asked.

"Yes," Ciyrs said with a laugh. "You can do the same thing that I can. You have the same power to heal. I've taught you to make the same potions. You have been able to help people in this compound just as much as I have."

"That's not true," Elianna said. "You've done far more. You've saved the lives of men who I never could have. I might know how to make the ointments, but you know them by heart. You can make them faster and stronger. You know how to make more of them than I do. You can control your healing far better than I can."

"That's only because you haven't been doing it for as long as I have," Ciyrs told her. "With practice, it will be easier and more natural to you. You will be able to do everything that I can, and possibly even more."

Elianna shook her head again.

"I'm not that special," she said. "Remember, Eden is a healer, too. She might not do it as often as we do, but she is able to perform healings and helped many of the people in the basement in the laboratory."

"Yes," Ciyrs said. "That's true. But she's not human. Remember that. When I saved her life, it was in exchange for her being human. The healing completely changed her DNA and turned her into a Denynso healer. It is a rare and special gift for the powers of a healer to be transferred to his mate during the bonding. It doesn't always happen, and it has never happened for a human woman. You are the only human woman to have the healing powers of a Denynso. You are truly and incredibly unique and every day I am more honored to have you beside me as my partner and as my mate."

Elianna pressed her lips to Ciyrs's again, sucking his bottom lip into her mouth before placing her hands on his hips to guide him back so that he leaned back against the table. She moved her mouth to his neck and kissed her way down as she brought her hands to the laces at the front of his shirt and released them. The fabric fell away beneath her fingers as she pushed away the sides to reveal his chest and taut, rippling belly. No matter how many times she saw this man without his clothing, she was intoxicated simply by the look of his exquisite body. It felt like it had been so long since she had been able to touch him and she couldn't resist the craving for him any longer.

Leaning against the table brought him down to a low enough height that by the time that she reached the middle of his neck Elianna was able to lower down off of the balls of her feet to continue her progress down his body with her lips. She felt Ciyrs sigh and his muscles relax as she kissed him and ran her hands down his stomach. When she glanced up at him, she saw that his eyes were closed. Elianna stepped back enough to let her release the fastening at the front of his pants and open them, releasing his hardening cock into her hand. She took it eagerly, wrapping her hand around the shaft so that she could stroke it. His erection hardened intensely beneath her touch, becoming thicker and more delectable-looking with each passing second.

As she stroked, Ciyrs's breath deepened and he relaxed further against the table, his thighs parting further to grant her greater access. Elianna lowered herself to her knees in front of him, bringing herself to the perfect height so that her face was even with his powerful erection. From this vantage point she could see the shimmering drop of fluid that was forming at the very tip and gliding down, welcoming her to touch him more. She brought her hand down to wrap firmly around the base of his shaft, positioning it so that it was primed for the attention that she craved giving him. Urging herself to move slowly, to savor every moment that she had, Elianna touched the tip of her tongue just above her hand and ran it up the underside of his cock, following the thick vein there. When she reached the engorged head, she traced the curve of the crown, pausing when she returned to the back to concentrate on the bundle of sensitive nerves at the top of the shaft.

Ciyrs groaned. Taking the pleased sound as an invitation, Elianna flicked her tongue along the slit at the tip of her mate's cock and let it dip in briefly. Finally, she opened her mouth, indulging her desire to taste him fully. He filled her mouth so completely that she could feel the tip of his erection pressing against her throat. She relaxed, allowing her tongue to swirl around his fullness as he slid partially into her throat. Ciyrs's hand touched her back, holding her in place as she continued to worship him. Her mouth slid along his length, her tongue stretching and curving to touch every ridge and vein so that there was not a single inch of him that wasn't given attention. Her hand continued to hold his shaft, making small, tight strokes to ensure that she was fully enveloping him as her mouth moved along him.

The sounds bubbling from Ciyrs's chest were delicious in Elianna's ears and she continued to suck, gradually increasing the depth and speed of her movements as she coaxed him toward oblivion. She wanted to give him everything, to offer him release that would, if only for a few moments, allow him to leave the tense, challenging space where his mind had been since they left the ship. Suddenly she felt his hands on her arms, squeezing just beneath her shoulders and pulling on her as if to guide her up. Elianna withdrew his cock from her mouth and stood, keeping her hand wrapped around him firmly, unwilling to let him go.

"What?" she asked. "Aren't you enjoying this?"

"Oh, I'm enjoying it," Ciyrs said breathlessly, "but I want more. I want to be inside you."

Elianna felt herself flush with the wave of arousal that flooded through her. She bit down on her bottom lip and ran her hand along his cock a few more times.

"I wanted something just for you," she said.

Ciyrs shook his head.

"I want something for both of us."

Elianna stepped back, reluctantly releasing his erection, and undressed. She kept her eyes focused on his, enjoying the way they seemed to darken slightly and slumber with desire for her. This was the man who had saved her life, and to whom she had then devoted it. When she was fully bare, Ciyrs stood and slipped his shirt back off of his shoulders and then stepped out of his pants. It felt like it had been so long since she had been able to be with him and she couldn't wait to feel his body against hers. Ciyrs climbed up so that he sat on the table and reached for her. Taking her by the waist, he lifted her up and onto his lap. She rested her hands on his shoulders and used them to hold her steady as he wrapped his arm around her hips and held her firmly. She felt him guide the tip of his erection toward her waiting core and stroke it into her warm, wet folds. It touched her taut, sensitive clit and she gasped, her head falling back as the sensation overtook her.

Ciyrs pressed his fingertips into her hip and pulled Elianna down, simultaneously guiding himself into her so that he sank all the way within her body in one deep thrust. Elianna settled into his lap, letting her thighs relax on either side of him so that he filled her completely. She started to sit forward, but Ciyrs flattened his hand into the center of her chest and guided her back so that she leaned slightly away from him. The position allowed him to run his hand down her chest and belly and into the valley between her thighs, reaching the place where their bodies met. Continuing to hold her tightly around the hips, Ciyrs turned his hand so that the pad of his thumb nestled onto her tight pearl.

Tightening his hips to thrust up into her, Ciyrs began to

stroke her in close circles, gradually increasing the intensity as he pushed harder and deeper into her. It suddenly didn't matter where they were or what had been happening around them. All that mattered to her was being in his arms and cradling him within her body. It was grounding and reassuring, soothing in its familiarity and empowering in its intensity. Here, she was safe, yet it also made her feel like she could face and conquer anything. This was everything.

Elianna gasped as she felt Ciyrs lean forward and capture one of her nipples in his mouth. His tongue swirled around it much like hers had on his erection and she arched harder into the sensation. The feeling shot through her body and into her core, heightening the sensation of his cock stroking with her. With every passing second his movements became faster and harder, more directed as they savored and celebrated each other. Elianna felt as though she was reaching the limit of her control, but she heard Ciyrs beginning to grunt, his sounds becoming more rhythmic.

Finally, Elianna couldn't control the feelings any longer. She gave herself over to them, crying out with release as all of the pressure throughout her body crashed around her in a cascade of contractions and tremors that drew Ciyrs deeper into her and embraced him harder. The feeling seemed to push him over his own edge and a few seconds later he grasped her hips with both hands and thrust up into her several hard times before growling with the hard pulse of his own release within her. Elianna dropped forward, draping her arms around his neck and resting her head on his shoulder. The smell of his skin was salty and comforting, lulling her even further. Ciyrs wrapped his arm around her waist again and held her tightly to him as he slid off of the edge of the table. Continuing to hold her up with his unimaginable strength, he leaned down and gathered their clothing off of the floor.

Elianna didn't move as he carried her out of the room through the door at the back and up the narrow flight of stairs that led to another floor of the building where they had set up their bedroom. This allowed them to be close to the main treatment room in the event that one of the wounded needed attention for their injuries or someone became sick in the night and needed to be transferred back to this treatment room for healing. Now, though, it was just reassuring for Elianna to know that they didn't have to go out of the building or cross the compound. All they needed to do was slip into the blankets that they had piled onto the hard cot they found there and go to sleep in each other's arms, ready to rejuvenate themselves for the next day.

9

———

"Are you thinking about them?"

Angela looked over her shoulder, slightly startled by the sound of Jem's voice. He walked up behind her and leaned down to wrap a blanket around her shoulders. She hadn't realized that she was cold, but now the weight and warmth of the blanket around her felt wonderful. She grasped either side of it and pulled it closer around her as Jem settled into place beside her.

"Thinking about who?" she asked.

Jem looked up at the sky toward the meager scattering of stars that she had been looking at. They were sharing the building that they had chosen to be their home while they were in the compound with two other warriors and when she found the small hatch that allowed her up onto the roof, she had felt like she had been given a small space of peace where she could be away from the noise and the chaos of the rest of the compound and all of those on it. It wasn't that she didn't want to be there or that she was regretting the decision that she had made, but she had become accustomed to the quiet of the planet that she shared with Jem and having so many people around her at all times had become overwhelming. Being able to sit on the roof, guarded from view by walls that rose several feet around all of the edges, gave her time to feel as though she could finally breathe.

"When you stare up at the stars like that, I always feel like you are thinking about the other people on the excavation team who went through the portal with you."

Angela let out a breath and turned her eyes back toward the stars. She was still getting used to having someone know her as well as Jem did, but there were moments like these where it was at once unfamiliar and incredibly reassuring. It made her feel more secure to know that he was there and that he seemed to be able to see what was within her, even if he didn't completely understand it. She nodded.

"Where are they?" she asked. "What could have happened to them? I know now that the portal sent us to different places, that we actually went through more than one portal, but where did they end up? I wish that I knew where they went and what they found when they got there."

"Is Jacob the only one that you saw again after the portal?" he asked.

"No," Angela said. "When Jacob and I were exploring the frozen stream that we ended up in, we found one of the others. He was already dead. One night I thought that I saw someone else running across the open field in front of our shelter, but when we chased them, we didn't find anyone. Jacob thought that I was just hallucinating because I was so cold, and we hadn't eaten in a few days."

"I hate that you went through that," Jem said.

She heard the tension in his voice that was always there

when they talked about the time that she and Jacob spent struggling to survive. He never resisted her talking about it or tried to get her to stop, but she knew that it hurt him to know everything that she had to suffer in the early times before they got used to being in the frozen, snowy world and learned to live.

"I know you do," she said, turning to rest her chin on her shoulder so that she could look at him. "I love you."

"I love you, too."

He leaned forward and kissed her softly.

"Sometimes I feel guilty for how easily I got through that," Angela admitted.

"What do you mean?" Jem asked. "You didn't get through those five years easily."

"But I got through them," she said. "I survived. I'm here. There are others who were standing there with me in that cavern who didn't. They never made it through those years. Even if there are some who did, they still haven't made it back to Earth. We have no idea where they are or what they might be dealing with right now. They could be suffering unimaginably and there's nothing that I can do to help them."

"You can't think about it that way," Jem told her. "You can't let yourself think about what they might be going through. Like you said, there is nothing that you can do for them. Besides, the planet that we shared was at the end of one of those portals. They might have found somewhere wonderful and are enjoying a new life now. Just think of that."

Angela smiled and nodded.

"I'd like to think that they are as happy as I am."

"Are you happy?" Jem asked.

"Of course, I am," she said. "I'm here with you. That makes me happier than anything else."

"But with all of this going on," he said, gesturing around them. "How are you dealing with it? I know this isn't what you expected when you said that you were going to come with me to help my kind back on Uoria."

"I didn't really know what to expect," Angela said. "All I cared about was getting you back to the Denynso and making sure that you could do for them what you know that you should."

"But now that we're here, are you sure that you made the right decision?"

"Any decision that ensured that I could be with you is the right decision. I'll admit, though, that this has been strange and overwhelming. After five years with only Jacob, this is so much more than I have been living with and some of it has been hard. At the same time, though, this is exactly the type of thing that I would have signed up for if I had had the opportunity before I went through the portal."

"It is?"

"Absolutely. If I had known that there was something like this happening and that I could be a part of it before I signed up to go on the research trip, I would have wanted to be a part of it. Unraveling something like this and being able to do my part to defend Earth and the rest of the Universe would have been exactly what I would have wanted to do if I had had the opportunity."

"Why did you decide to be a part of the research project?" Jem asked.

"It was something to do," Angela said. "I know that's an awful response and it makes me sound useless, but it's the truth. I wanted to do more. I wanted to do something impactful. But I wasn't in the University, so I couldn't be a part of any of the departments that handled any intergalactic projects or even excavations on other planets. Working in the research halls and attempting to recreate sites had become so incredibly tedious. I needed to do something else. I needed to feel like I was actually doing something that mattered. The HM-1313 wall was a major discovery and it raised so many questions about our understanding of the ancient civilizations. I knew that there was more to it than our existing understanding and I thought that if I was a part of the excavation, maybe I could uncover something."

"Well, you certainly achieved that."

Angela chuckled.

"That is definitely true. That portal was something that I never would have expected, but I suppose it was exactly what I was looking for. I made an impact. I just didn't know how at the time."

"How did you survive?" Jem asked. "You had so little with you."

"I barely know myself," Angela said. "It was necessary. We survived because we had to. It was so hard at first. There were plenty of moments that I didn't think that we were going to make it. I didn't know how we were going to find the shelter that we needed or how we were going to eat. As much as I had wanted to get away from the tedium of my life, I wanted nothing more than to get back to it. I couldn't imagine carrying on in a world like that, especially with only Jacob to see me through. But then we did. We kept going. We learned new skills and we discovered strength inside of ourselves that we didn't know we had. We kept going for the same reason that I can now tell you that we survived. Because we had to. It got easier over time. Then I met Galadriel and Vyker."

"I didn't get much of a chance to interact with them," Jem said. "What little time we were together we were too focused on what we were trying to do to really get to know each other. What were they like?"

"I didn't know them well," Angela said. "They were intense. I remember that. Driven. It was obvious how much they loved each other, but they were so focused on finding the stones that Vyker needed. They helped us out of the frozen stream and brought us back to Vyker's stream."

"It seems strange to talk about them like that," Jem said.

"Like what?" Angela asked.

"In the past tense. Like they don't exist anymore."

"In this time, in this stream, they don't, Jem. I know that it's hard to think about, but in this reality, they have been dead for many years. I've come to terms with that, but..." her voice trailed off and she felt unsure of whether she wanted to continue the thought.

"But what?" Jem asked. "Tell me."

She sighed and looked up at the stars again, remembering what Galadriel and Vyker had told her about the origins of the stars and the lives that they represented. Here on Penthos there were so few stars, the pinpricks in the sky even seeming paler and less sparkling than they did on Earth or on the planet that she and Jem had shared. It was a stark reminder, a painful underscore of what she knew about Galadriel and Vyker, and what she had begun to think of herself.

"What does that mean for me when I was in the frozen realm? I don't know when or where that realm was. It could have been far into the future or even further in the past than Vyker's stream. So, when I was there, for those five years that

I lived in the snow and the ice – was I dead, or I had not even been born?"

It was a painful thought that she hadn't put voice to until that moment and Angela didn't know how Jem was going to respond. She looked up at him and saw him gazing at her with his intense orange eyes, the shade so vibrant and unusual, and yet so familiar to her now. Finally, he spoke.

"When I first arrived on the other planet, I had no idea where I was. I didn't know what had happened or what I was supposed to do. Growing up in the Denynso compound, I was always with the rest of my kind. We ate together every day. We trained together from the time that we were young children. We spent nearly all of our time together. The concept of being along for any length of time was something completely foreign to me. Then suddenly found myself totally and utterly alone. There was no one else on the planet as far as I knew, and the longer that I searched, the emptier and alone the planet felt. It didn't take long for me to realize that not only was I far away from Uoria, but that the clan was going to think that I had died. They had no way of knowing that I had just somehow been transported to another planet and that I was fine but didn't have a way to get back to them. I knew that in their minds and in their hearts, I had died in that battle. Then that was how I began to feel. If they thought that I was dead and in their hearts believed that I was, then for all intents and purposes, I was dead. I no longer had the life that I had been living or the life that I thought that I would live into the future. So, what did I have?"

"But you were still alive," Angela protested. "You had simply found another, amazing planet and were doing just fine on your own. By the time that I got there, you had already established so much of a life there. It was almost as though you had been there all along."

"Yet everyone on Uoria still thought that I was dead. The point is that you don't have to rely on the perceptions and beliefs of others. All that matters is what you are experiencing. When you were in that frozen stream, you existed. You were alive. It doesn't matter what time or place it was, because you were nowhere but there. People here might not have known where you were or what happened to you, and the other members of the team that disappeared at the same time might have even thought that you were dead, but that doesn't matter. That doesn't make any impact on what really happened or your existence. I can promise you, though. You will never have to question anything about yourself or your existence ever again. You are here with me now and as long as we are together, there is nothing that can ever make us question ourselves."

"What are we going to do when this is all over?" Angela asked.

"What do you mean?" Jem asked.

"We never talked about what we were going to do when we found your kind on Uoria. When all of this is over. When the war is over and Ryan has been taken out of power, what are we going to do?"

"What do you want to do?"

"At first, when we were on the jungle planet together, I thought that that was it. I had resigned myself to the reality that I wasn't going to go back to Earth and that we were going to live out of lives together there. Even before you and I got together, I was contented to be there and to discover a new life. But now that we've been able to move so easily between the streams, I'm more conflicted."

"Why?"

"There's so much possibility out here, Jem. There's so much that I've never seen or done, so much that I could never have even imagined. I love what we were creating there on our planet together, but I don't know anymore if that is enough to keep me fulfilled." She looked at him with worry, concerned that he might misunderstand what she was saying. "Please don't think that I mean that I don't want to be with you or that I no longer like the home that we built together there."

"No," Jem said. "It's alright. I understand. It's the same way that I feel about the Denynso compound on Uoria."

"It is?"

Jem nodded.

"The warriors never left the compound. At least not in my lifetime. We were expected to stay there and to live our lives in battle, protecting the compound and the rest of Uoria. That was something that I never questioned or thought strange. Then I was transported to our planet and saw that there was so much more to the Universe than just the compound. That doesn't mean that I don't love the compound where I grew up or being with my kind, but it does mean that I can't imagine going through the rest of my life staying within the confines of that stone wall. I need to do more, to see more, to feel as though I'm making more of a difference than I could just being there. I can't expect any less of you." Angela saw his eyes scan her face more closely. "Do you want to return to Earth when all of this is done? Go back to your life there and try to put it back together?"

Angela sighed and shook her head.

"I have no idea," she said. "I can't even imagine what it would be like to go back there and try to live that life again. What would I do when I got there? The company told my family and everyone who knew me some story about where

I went. What would I tell them? Would I go along with what the company said and try to keep that going, or would I tell them the truth about what happened and where I've been? Is there any way that I could even explain it? How do you go about telling someone that they've been lied to for five years and that what really happened to you is far more difficult to understand than anything that they could ever imagine? I don't even know if that's what I would want. I've gotten used to being away from Earth and everything and everyone that I've ever known. Would I even go see my family? If I did, would they accept me and my explanation? Would I even want them to?"

"I can't answer those questions for you," Jem said. "I don't know what would be right. I wasn't gone from Uoria as long as you were gone from Earth, but I know that it was difficult for me to think about facing the clan and trying to explain what happened to me. I knew that they thought that I was dead and that they had gone through the mourning process for me. Encountering them again and trying to explain seemed impossible, but it was something that I had to do. You have a very different situation, though, and I don't know what's right for you."

A painful thought went through Angela's mind and she felt her body draw closer to his.

"If I did want to go back to Earth," she started cautiously, "would you consider going with me?"

"Of course, I would," Jem said without hesitation. "I would go anywhere with you. There is nothing that would keep me from wanting to be with you and from doing anything that I could to be with you."

"I guess there isn't really any point in me thinking about it now," Angela said. "We're stuck here and there's nothing that we can do about it until this is all over."

Jem wrapped his arm around her shoulders and drew her up against him so that he could hold her. She felt him kiss the side of her head and rest his forehead against her.

"We'll make it through this," he said reassuringly. "For now, let's just focus on what is in front of us right now and then when the time comes, we can decide what to do from there."

10

Jonah watched as Nana pushed a few of the files around on the top of her desk, looking at their covers and occasionally opening them to glance in at their front pages. She had been doing this for several minutes, not saying anything, but seeming absorbed in what she was seeing even if she was doing little to really investigate the files and their contents.

"Do you understand any of this?" Aubrey finally asked. "Does any of this make sense to you?"

"I don't know what you're asking me, Aubrey," Nana said. "Why would I understand any of this? These are files from before I was even born."

"I know that," Aubrey said. "That's the point. These all come from more than a hundred years ago, and yet this one, this one right here is *my* file. It says that I went to the University medical ward three times and saw different doctors. There's also a page missing from it that could have anything on it, and we don't know. How is this possible?"

"Why are you asking me about it?"

There was something strange in Nana's voice, something

just beneath the words that Jonah could detect but couldn't quite decipher. It was as though she wasn't really asking the question to get an actual answer that would clarify the situation for her, but rather that she was asking just to see what Aubrey and he were going to say to her.

"I think you know why," Aubrey said. "You know who Jonah is. You are the one who gave me that book that would tell me who he is. Why was that book so important?"

"I told you, it belonged to my mother. She loved that book and we spent a lot of time going through it together."

"I know that's what you told me," Aubrey continued, "but you didn't explain why it was so important. Why did your mother put so much value into it?"

"And why did she spend so much time touching my picture?" Jonah asked.

Both women looked up at him as if they had almost forgotten that he was there with them.

"She was a very private woman," Nana said. "Whatever was happening in her mind and heart when she was touching that picture stayed there. All of my memories of my mother have that book in them. It was her most precious possession."

Jonah looked at Nana and she met his eyes, the expression in them seeming to convey something within her that she didn't want to say. He gave a slight nod and turned to Aubrey.

"The book," he said. "We've gone through all of this because of that book, but we didn't even think about looking at the book itself. You used that to find out about me, so why don't we use it to find out more?"

Aubrey's eyes widened.

"We can read the book. Maybe it will give us some insight into what is going on here. That book was written just a few years after the Nyx 23 crew went missing. It has a different perspective than the books that are written about it now."

"Exactly," Jonah said. "It was written by people who were actually around when the entire situation happened. It can tell us things about what everyone knew and how they felt about it that we can't get from reading contemporary books, and at the same time, the contemporary books might tell us more or different things that the older book doesn't. If we read the old book, we can compare what's in it to what you learned about the situation in school and I can tell you want actually happened."

Aubrey nodded.

"It's pretty clear that the accuracy of the information that was shared with the public is fairly suspect. If we can compare all of the different views, maybe they will overlap or contrast distinctly and something will stand out that will make something make sense."

Jonah didn't know what they might find in the old book or how it might further illuminate the situation, but it was all that they could think of to do. Aubrey rushed out of the room to get the book and Jonah turned to look at Nana.

"You always knew who I was," he said.

Nana gave a slow nod.

"From the moment that I saw you walk in the door. I can't forget your face. It's one I have seen so many times before. I just never could have imagined that this would be the way that I would see it again."

"You have to know something, Nana. Something about this has to make sense to you."

Before the older woman could answer him, Aubrey ran through the office door again, gripping the book tightly against her chest. She closed the door behind her and stepped up to the desk. Placing the book on it, she pulled a chair up and sat down. Jonah followed her lead and they both leaned forward over the desk to look at it. Aubrey flipped the cover and the book immediately opened to the page of pictures of the crew. Jonah's eyes locked on his own face again, noticing now the change in texture of the page that indicated just how much Nana's mother touched this image of him. It was a strange thought and one that he didn't know how to feel about. At once, it was nice to know that there was someone who had thought so much of him even then, long after he was lost and the world thought that he had died. At the same time, however, he didn't know Nana's mother and didn't understand the draw that she would have had to him. This made her obvious attachment to him feel like it somewhat threw him off balance.

Jonah took his eyes away from the picture of himself to look at the faces of the rest of the crew, emotion starting to coil in his stomach as he saw the images of those who had been lost in the crash and those he had left behind when he chose to come with the crew to Earth. He had looked at nearly all of them when something struck him. He scanned back over the pictures again, pulling the book closer to look at them more intently.

"What is it?" Aubrey asked.

Jonah picked up the book and flipped to the back so he could look through the resource section. He looked at the picture again and then compared it to the information that he found. After a few seconds he put the book back down on the desk and pointed at the picture of a smiling man at the center of the bank of pictures.

"Him," Jonah said. "This man. I don't know him."

Aubrey turned the book toward herself and looked down at the picture.

"What do you mean you don't know him?" she asked. "That's the pilot of the StarCity."

Jonah shook his head.

"No. I know that's what it says, but that's not him."

"I don't understand," Aubrey said. "This is Martin Roe, the man who is always credited with being the pilot for the Nyx 23 mission. He's in all of the textbooks and all of the research about the mission. It says that he was one of the most clandestine of the people included on the mission because of his work outside of the program. His family didn't even know that he was a part of the project until after the crew went missing. He was given full honors at the memorial service held in his honor."

"Memorial service?" Jonah asked.

Aubrey nodded.

"Once it was fully established that the ship had gone missing and was no longer in communication with mission control, the military and government decided that they would do a search of the planet and the surrounding areas to try to find any clues that might indicate where the ship went and if any of the crew was still alive. After the military recognizance groups returned without any word of what happened, the planet entered into a formal waiting period. When that was over, the entire crew was declared dead. There were memorial services for everyone and a national day of mourning was established."

"A memorial service was held for me?" Jonah asked.

Aubrey nodded.

"Yes. There were huge funeral rituals and speeches. Nyx 23 became the martyrs of the entire planet. People used the situation to call for stricter intergalactic cooperation and laws, and others demanded that Earth shut off all alliances with planets that weren't deemed occupied and civilized for more than 50 years. It became really heated. Remembering Nyx 23 became a rallying cry for all kinds of demands and changes in policy and protocol."

"Can you show me pictures of the memorial services?" Jonah asked.

"I can do something even better than that," Aubrey said. She crossed the room to one of the large bookshelves that lined one wall. "These are my textbooks from college. By the time that I was in school, the high school studies of the disaster were fairly cursory. They covered what happened and the effects of it, but it didn't get into as much detail. In college, though, the research was much more extensive. I took a class that devoted almost three weeks just to the disappearance and the after-affects. This book," she pulled a book down from the shelf and carried it over to the desk, "is considered one of the foremost texts on the topic. It has first-hand accounts, blueprints...but it also has this."

Aubrey opened the book to a page that was entirely taken up by the image of a large crowd looking up at an elevated stage. The back of the stage was filled with massive floral displays while the center held a pedestal with a man standing behind it. He was gesturing toward the crowd and Jonah could see that there was a long row of empty chairs positioned along either side of the stage as well as on another platform in front.

"What is this?" Jonah asked.

"It's the memorial service that was held for the entire crew."

Jonah watched as Aubrey touched a dark spot at the bottom of the picture and a shimmering blue and white hologram rose out of the picture. He was surprised that the technology had been integrated into a textbook, but when it started moving and sound came toward him, all other thoughts left his mind. He listened intently as the man, who Jonah soon recognized as a military leader, addressed the crowd, telling them about the bravery and sacrifice of the Nyx 23 crew. He talked about the clandestine nature of the project and reassured the public that this was intended as protection for them and for the planet. They didn't want to cause panic or disrupt the normal progression of people's lives for something that was still in exploratory stages and would hopefully have no direct impact on the people of Earth. He was poetic and emotional, calling upon all of those on Earth and on all allied planets to never forget those who had lost their lives in their effort to protect not just the people of Earth, but the values and truths that all those who were aligned with the intergalactic agreements held dear.

Jonah felt strangely breathless as he watched the memorial service unfold with music and further speeches. As the program drew to a close, the leader stepped behind the pedestal again and announced that they would complete the memorial service by reading out the names of the crew members along with displaying their images. The crowd fell silent again and a valiant, almost triumphant song rose up along with the first image of a crew member. Jonah, Aubrey, and Nana remained in silence, as though suspended in the moment along with the rest of the crowd, watching reverently as the faces of the crew slid past and the sound of their names reverberated through the stillness. Aubrey walked around to Jonah's side and he felt her take his hand, squeezing it comfortingly as they went deeper into the list. He shuddered slightly as his face appeared in the hologram and the man called his name, returning the squeeze of Aubrey's hand.

They had gone through dozens of names when there

was a slight pause and the man gestured toward the screen where the images had appeared.

"Of course, all of the souls on this crew were led fearlessly by their courageous and devoted pilot, Martin Roe."

"That," Jonah said, pointing at the hologram. "That's not right. There was no Martin Roe on the crew. He wasn't with us."

The hologram had gone still, and Aubrey touched the button again to close it out.

"What do you mean it isn't right? Why would they memorialize someone as the pilot of a crew when he wasn't even there?"

"I don't know, but I can tell you that that man was not our pilot. I was there, remember? I knew every person on the primary crew. I didn't know the names of all of the mechanical crew, but I knew the pilot. His name was Etan, not Martin Roe, and he didn't look anything like that picture that they just showed. I spent months training alongside Etan and weeks onboard the StarCity with him. I know what I'm talking about."

"I just don't understand," Aubrey said. "How is that possible? How could they not know that they were memorializing the wrong pilot? How could they write about him and teach that he was the pilot for all of these years?"

"I don't know," Jonah said, "but I think that there is a far more pressing question than that."

"Who is Martin Roe and why did no one notice that he was being credited for piloting a mission that he had nothing to do with?"

Jonah nodded at Nana.

"He had to have a family. Colleagues. Friends. Something. Someone had to notice that he was being lauded as the fearless leader of the StarCity when he didn't go at all.

Someone had to notice that he was still on Earth, alive and well, even after the mission was said to have disappeared."

"Like him," Aubrey said. "Where did he go? If he didn't have anything to do with this mission, or if he was supposed to but then changed his mind, why didn't he say anything? Why didn't he come forward and point out that he wasn't on the ship at all, much less when it disappeared? No one said anything about him or his life after the mission, so what happened to him?"

"I think that we need to go to the factory," Jonah said.

"The Izalux factory?" Nana asked.

Jonah nodded and started to gather the patient files.

"I know that it doesn't make any sense right now, but it's all the connection that we have right now. We need to get to that factory and find out anything else that we can."

"I'll call the lab and tell them that I'm going to need a leave of absence," Aubrey said. "Considering I haven't even taken vacation in the entire time that I've worked there and today is my first sick day in three years, I think that they owe me a little bit of time without too many complaints."

"I'll go up and start packing," Jonah said. "We have some research that we need to do before we go, but I want to make sure that we are ready as soon as possible."

NANA WATCHED as Aubrey and Jonah rushed out of the office and went in different directions, readying themselves for the challenge that was in front of them. She drew in a breath and stood slowly. Her body suddenly felt older and heavier as she walked around the large desk toward the door to the office. Everything felt like it was rushing toward her, moments that she had anticipated for years suddenly happening though she hadn't yet prepared herself for them. She climbed the back stairs that led up to her bedroom and closed the door behind her, closing out the sound of the muffled voices that were rising up toward her from the floor below. She leaned back against the door for a few seconds, gathering her thoughts and emotions, before crossing the room to her vanity and the antique jewelry box sitting there.

Her hands trembled slightly as she opened the box and removed the insert that concealed a hidden panel. Nana reached into a ring box on the other side of the vanity table and withdrew a tiny key that she used to unlock the panel and moved the polished cherry wood slat aside. Returning the key to its place, she reached into the compartment and withdrew a small stack of letters. The thick envelopes crackled in her hands as she held them, their musty smell and dry texture revealing their age.

After a few seconds, she pulled the letters away from her heart where she had been holding them and looked down at the willowy script across the front of the top letter. It was the same on each of the envelopes, her name swept across the thick, creamy paper in fading blue ink. The only difference in the envelopes was the instructions written on the back of the flap of each. None had been opened, all left completely sealed just as they were when she found them in the days following her mother's death. They were tucked in that compartment in the jewelry box, unopened, seemingly untouched from when they were placed there. She could only assume that they had been written by her mother years before her death, years even before Nana's birth. Though her curiosity had nearly overcome her, she had forced herself to resist opening the envelopes, telling herself that she had to follow the guidelines that were written on the back of the envelopes, knowing that she was only to open them when the notes on the envelope flaps dictated.

Nana slipped the envelopes back into the hidden compartment of the jewelry box and rested her hand on them for a few moments. She knew that the time was coming to open them and she would finally know exactly what they said. In her heart, she knew what the letters were about. It could only be one thing, only one mystery that could be important enough for her mother to put the effort into writing the letters and keeping them concealed throughout Nana's life to ensure that she would open them at just the right moment.

Closing the compartment, Nana picked up the tiny key again and locked it before placing the insert back into place. She returned the jewelry box to its position on the vanity table and then took the few steps to the small bookshelf on the other side of the room. A silver picture frame stood out in stark contrast from the faded antique books that surrounded it. She reached for it and took it into her hands. The faces of her parents gazed up at her and she looked down at them with a blend of love and sadness in her heart. Nana touched each of them, first tracing the outline of her father's face and then her mother's. She could still remember them so distinctly, from the sound of their voices to the smell of their skin when they hugged her. When she closed her eyes, she could still feel the soft fabric of her father's shirt when he lifted her into his arms and carried around the house after coming home from work, or her mother's hand brushing across her hair as she lulled her to sleep at night.

"It's all working out now," Nana whispered to the picture. "It's all going to be fine. I'll make sure that it is."

11

Gannon walked through the front door of Nana's house and immediately sensed the frantic, almost chaotic energy that was in the air. It was the first time that he had been back to the house in a couple of days and it felt as though something within the walls had shifted. He paused just inside the door and looked around, waiting for something to happen, though he didn't know what.

"Is something wrong?" Willow asked from behind him.

Gannon shook his head, not wanting to alarm her. There was still so much about himself and everything that he had been through that he hadn't told her yet and that she wouldn't understand. It wasn't that he didn't want her to know or that he was ashamed of what he had been through. He knew that in time he would be able to tell her everything and it would draw them closer together. For now, though, they were still building their relationship, exploring their newfound love as they got to know each other. He didn't know what might be happening in the house, but there was worry in the back of his mind that it had something to do with Ryan. Gannon didn't want to risk putting Willow into any kind of danger, so he glanced over his shoulder toward her and smiled.

"No," he said. "Everything's fine. I think everybody's still sleeping."

Willow glanced down at her phone.

"At this hour?" she asked. "At least Aubrey shouldn't be. She should be getting ready for work. And I should, too." She leaned forward and kissed him. "I'll see you tonight?" she asked.

"Absolutely."

Gannon kissed her again, never feeling like he could get enough of the feeling or taste of her lips. He wanted to sweep her up into his arms and spend the day holding her, but he knew that she couldn't. Willow gave him another smile.

"Tell Nana that I came by, but I didn't have much time."

"I will."

A final kiss and she left, walking back down the front stairs and to her car where she had left it in the driveway. As soon as she had driven away, Gannon stepped the rest of the way into the house and closed the door behind him. He could hear footsteps above him and knew that there was someone else awake in the house. He climbed the stairs cautiously, unsure of what he was going to encounter when he got there. When he stepped onto the landing, he saw a figure rushing out of a room toward him. The automatic defensiveness swelled in him and Gannon felt primed to fight, but an instant later he realized that it was Jonah coming out of his bedroom.

Gannon's muscles released, and he chided himself for still not being able to control the urges that were within him. He wanted to free himself of them, to remove them from his mind so that he could live his life without always waiting for the next attack, the next imagined battle.

"What are you doing?" he asked as Jonah continued past him and started down the stairs.

Jonah looked back at him, but didn't answer. Gannon followed him down the stairs and watched as he placed two large suitcases that he had been carrying beside the front door.

"Did anyone see you while you were gone?" Jonah asked.

"Just Willow," Gannon replied. "Are you going somewhere?"

Jonah looked at Gannon for a few moments as if evaluating him and then gestured toward the stairs.

"Come with me."

They rushed up the steps and into one of the small rooms off of the hallway that led to Jonah's bedroom. Inside Aubrey was sitting at a table tucked into the curve of a large bay window. There were papers and books spread in front of her and she was holding a computerized map in her hands. She looked up when they walked in and then glanced at Jonah questioningly.

"What is he doing here?" she asked.

Jonah gestured toward the table and they both sat down with Aubrey.

"There's something that neither of us thought about," he said. "We've been looking through these files and books and trying to figure out what these people were thinking, but we never stopped to think of the unique perspective into all of this that we have had right in front of us." He looked at Gannon. "A glimpse into the mind of the continuation of what started with Nyx 23."

Gannon didn't understand what Jonah was talking about, but he could tell by the looks on both of their faces that they considered him extremely important to whatever it was that they were doing.

"Gannon," Aubrey said, leaning slightly toward him across the table. "Do you know anything about something called Izalux?"

The word tumbled around in Gannon's mind, but he couldn't connect it to any memories or meaning. He shook his head.

"I've never heard of it," he said. "What is it?"

Aubrey looked back down at the papers and books in front of her and raked her fingers back through her hair.

"That's exactly what we're trying to figure out," she said.

"Can you tell us more about the Valdicians?" Jonah asked. "Anything? What they look like, any words that they used that you didn't hear anyone else use? Where they come from? Anything?"

Gannon shook his head.

"I don't know what I could tell you that would help you, or that you don't know already. We only saw them in their robes, just like you did. I can't tell you if they used any strange words because those are the words that we always heard." A thought crossed his mind and he stood. "Give me just a minute. I'll be right back."

He hurried out of the room and up the second flight of stairs to the bedrooms on the next floor. Rapping on the first door with his knuckles, Gannon leaned close to listen for any sound from inside. Finally, he heard footsteps coming toward him.

"Who is it?" a sleepy, suspicious voice asked from the other side of the door.

It was an expected response, one that Gannon knew that he was likely to give. Both still feared the possibility of the danger that they had left behind in the University reappearing and neither was fully ready to give up the guards that protected them.

"Mordecai, it's Gannon. I need to talk to you."

It was still strange to refer to the other hybrid man by the name that he had chosen, yet it felt completely natural for Gannon to think of himself with his own title. He knew that he was going to get used to it the more often he used it, and he was committed to saying it as much as he could, reinforcing it in his mind and in Mordecai's, railing against Ryan with every time that the sounds repeated in his mind and passed his lips.

A few seconds later the door opened and Mordecai peered out at him. He looked up and down the hallway and then eased his way around the door to step out with Gannon.

"What is it?" Mordecai asked.

"I don't think that we should talk here," Gannon said. "Come with me."

They made their way back to the room with Aubrey and sat at the table with her.

"They asked me about Izalux," Gannon said to Mordecai. "Have you ever heard that word? Do you know what it is?"

Mordecai shook his head.

"No, I..." Gannon saw his eyes widen and Mordecai leaned forward slightly. "Yes, he said. I have. I just remembered. One time when I was in reprogramming, I heard the Valdicians talking. I'm sure they didn't think that I could hear them or that I wasn't paying attention because of what I was going through, but I had already been reprogrammed so many times. I had learned to block out the process and focus my energy and attention on other things that were happening around me. This was before they implemented the screens."

Gannon felt himself shudder at the mention of the screens. He remembered how it felt to have them secured to his head and the horrific images that would flash in front of him for as long as the Valdicians kept him trapped in the reprogramming room. He wished that he could rid himself of those memories, that he could erase them from his mind and never have to think of them again. The pictures were like scars, though, branded into his mind so that he was never able to separate from them. Every moment of that was a part of him and he was going to have to learn to live with these existences in parallel, hoping that one day, the former fell away with the strength of his new life.

"What did they say?" Gannon asked.

"I heard one of them mention to another that they were running low on their supply."

"Of Izalux?" Aubrey asked.

Mordecai nodded.

"I think that's what they said. He said that they would need to go back to the factory where the storage was held to make sure that they had enough."

"But they didn't say what it was or what it did?" Jonah asked.

"No," Mordecai said. "They just said that they needed to go back to the factory. As they were leaving the room they were talking about how many of them would go and how much of the Izalux they would need to bring back with them to make sure that those who weren't able to make the journey with them had what they needed."

"We need to hurry," Jonah said, looking to Aubrey.

"Hurry?" Gannon asked. "Why? What are you doing?"

Aubrey looked at him, but didn't answer. She moved the

tip of her finger across the screen of the computerized map in her hand and then drew her fingers across it to isolate a certain part of the image.

"Are you going to the factory that the Valdicians mentioned?" Gannon asked. "Do you know where it is?"

Aubrey looked over Gannon toward Jonah.

"Did you finish packing?"

"Yes," Jonah said. "Are you sure that the lab isn't going to be expecting you?"

"When I called them yesterday I said that I was going to need at least two weeks."

"And if you aren't ready to go back in two weeks?"

"Then I don't go back."

"You are going to the factory," Gannon said. "What is it that you think that you're going to find there?"

Aubrey continued to ignore him as she gathered up everything that was on the table in front of her, but Jonah looked at him and nodded.

"We're going to the factory," he said. "We don't know what we're looking for or what we think that we might find. But this is all we have."

That was that Gannon needed to hear. He stood and extended his hand toward Jonah.

"I would be honored to go with you if you will have me," he said.

"You will?"

"You rescued me without question. I'm going to do the same. Whatever it is that you are looking for, or that you need to do, I will be there to help you."

"So will I," Mordecai offered.

Gannon saw Aubrey look between the two men and then met his eyes.

"Thank you," she said.

"Don't go."

The sound of the woman's voice stopped him before he was able to respond to Aubrey and they all turned toward it. Gannon saw Ilya standing at the doorway and realized that he and Mordecai hadn't closed the door when they had come back into the room. Her hand rested on her swollen belly, Ilya stepped the rest of the way into the room and looked at each of them pointedly.

"You can't go to the factory," Ilya said. "It's far too dangerous."

"What do you mean?" Jonah asked. "How do you know that the factory is dangerous?"

The woman gave what sounded like an exasperated sigh.

"Because I know," she said. "You need to stay away from there. Things happen there; you don't want to be a part of them."

"Why would you say that?" Aubrey asked.

Ilya turned toward Aubrey and gave her a look that bordered somewhere between smug and incredulous.

"Because I've been there."

12

Ilya couldn't believe that Aubrey was looking at her as though she had never seen her before. It was frustrating and almost infuriating in a way that Ilya couldn't quite put into words.

"You've been to the Izalux factory?" Aubrey asked.

"It's the Orion Corporation factory," Ilya said, "but yes, I have. But you already knew that, Aubrey."

Ilya saw Aubrey's face change as she went through a series of emotions in response to what she had said. At first, she seemed confused, almost repelled, by the assertion, but then slow realization washed over her and her expression relaxed as her eyes widened. She took a small step toward Ilya.

"You," she said softly. "You were in the lab."

Ilya nodded.

"I was," she said. "I didn't think that you would remember."

"I didn't," Aubrey admitted. "I didn't recognize you when I saw you. You were barely noticeable when you were in the lab."

"Well, thank you."

"No," Aubrey said. "That's not what I meant. I'm sorry. It's just—you were so quiet. You kept totally to yourself. I never even saw you talking to anyone else. You were working on a different project, so I didn't get a chance to interact with you. But I remember you. I remember you being there."

"Do you remember me leaving?"

Aubrey nodded and took another step toward her.

"I do," she said, her voice still softened as if she had forgotten that there was anyone else in the room with them and she was only speaking directly to Ilya. "You were there one day and then the next, you were just gone. There was a little bit of an upheaval because nobody could figure out what had happened to you. You hadn't let anyone know that you weren't going to be coming back in and no one knew how to get in touch with you, so we couldn't check in on you. After a few days, though, we all just assumed that you had found another job somewhere else and hadn't told anyone because you didn't really socialize with anyone so there wasn't anything to say. Those who were working on the same project that you were said that one of the very few things that they knew about you was that you didn't have any family."

"That's true," Ilya said. "I didn't have anybody. It's easy for someone to just disappear without anyone noticing when they don't have anyone in their lives to care that they are gone. That's what made it so easy for them to capture me and put me in the program. No one missed me when I was gone, so no one came looking for me."

"That's not true," Aubrey said. "We did wonder where you were, but there was nothing that we could do. You didn't have any contact information on file and since you didn't socialize with anyone there was no way for us to get in contact with you or to check to make sure that you were really alright. We couldn't look for you. Besides, there was someone in the lab who said that they heard you were dating someone."

"They did?" Ilya asked, taken aback by the revelation.

"Yes," Aubrey said. "They said that you had been seeing someone for a while, but that you were being quiet about it just like you were quiet about everything else. We figured that even with as quiet as you were, there would be some kind of indication that you were dating someone if there wasn't something wrong with the relationship. He would have come to the lab to visit you or you would have eaten with him some time rather than always bringing your lunch. It wasn't until you disappeared that we started to wonder if maybe you were dating someone who was in the University. Since being involved with someone in certain positions or departments wasn't allowed, you would have to be quiet about the relationship. We thought that maybe someone in their department or their superior found out about the relationship and threatened consequences, so the two of you ran off together."

Ilya was surprised. She didn't think that the people who had shared the same lab before she was captured even recognized that she existed a lot of the time, much less cared enough to go to that much trouble to think of reasons why she might have disappeared. While it felt like an invasion of her privacy for them to be conjecturing about her personal life and the motivations behind her leaving, it was also reassuring that they at least noticed that she was gone. She didn't want to go any further into what had happened, but she knew that she needed to. The only chance that she might have to convince them to stay away from the factory was to tell them what she had gone through. She nodded.

"I was seeing someone," she admitted.

"Was he a part of the University?" Aubrey asked.

Ilya looked into the faces of each of the people in the room, wanting to make sure that they were listening.

"Yes," she said. "It was Ryan."

Shocked gasps filled the room around her and Aubrey knew that her revelation had had the impact that she wanted it to. It wasn't something that she wanted to talk about. In all truth, it was something that she didn't even want to think about any longer. If she could completely eradicate him from her memory, she would. In that moment, however, he was virtually all that she could think about.

"You were involved with Ryan?" Aubrey asked, her voice sounding stunned.

Ilya felt a hard kick on the side of her belly and involuntarily pressed her hand against it. She felt Jonah take her by the arm and start guiding her back toward the chairs positioned around the table in the window.

"Sit down," he instructed. "Relax."

"Thank you," Ilya said.

The feeling of the sun on her skin, even through the glistening-clean window panes, was wonderful. It had been nearly a year since she had been able to be out in the sun and simply savor its warmth and beauty.

Aubrey and the men settled into chairs around her and she could feel them looking at her expectantly. They wanted to know more, and even though she was reluctant to share it, she took a breath and forced herself to say the words that they needed to hear.

"He was one of the assigned mentors during a project

that I did when I was studying at the University," she started. "We had a good rapport then and I was pretty disappointed when the project ended and I wasn't able to see him every day anymore."

"How could you be so attracted to him?" Aubrey asked.

"Ryan is far more charming than you give him credit for," Ilya said. "Besides, there was no way of knowing anything that he was doing. It wasn't as though he talked about it. He was kind and attentive and flattering. I liked the attention. I hate to even say that now. It makes me feel so incredibly stupid that I fell for it."

"You don't need to feel stupid," Aubrey said.

"Don't you think that I had heard all of the rumors about Ryan?" she asked. "I had heard everything that people said about him. I was fully informed of the type of man he was, and yet I still let myself be attracted to him like some little puppy. It was like I thought I was somehow special."

"So, what happened? Were you seeing him from the time that you were in that project?"

Ilya shook her head.

"No," she said. "After that project, I didn't see him for another couple of years. Then I started working in the lab and I ran into him again. Of course, I was thrilled to see him and he seemed really happy to see me, too. He told me that he had been thinking about me since we had worked together and that he had been hoping that we would have the opportunity to work together again. That just swept me away even more. He had just been my mentor and yet he talked about it as though we had made some sort of incredible discovery together. I was standing there with this powerful, famous scientist telling me that I impress him and that he wanted to be able to work with me. There was nothing that I could do. I couldn't resist him."

"Were you serious?" Aubrey asked. "Is that what happened? Did the Science Head find out about the two of you and threaten him?"

Ilya shook her head.

"No," she said. "Nothing that dramatic. We were actually quite casual. We saw each other when we had the chance. We would grab dinner or sometimes take a weekend together. I wish I had just left it at that and allowed it to fizzle out naturally, but I just couldn't. The longer that I spent with him, the less that I could resist him. I fell harder every time that I saw him. Even though I was still hearing the same rumors about him, I wanted to be more serious. I thought that I could change his ways and convince him that I was the one he was supposed to be with. No matter what I heard, I thought that I could be the one who was different. I just had to convince him. I had to show him that I could make him happy. When I told him, though, he didn't feel the same way."

"What did he say?"

Ilya sighed.

"Basically, what you would expect him to. That I was great and that he had fun with me, but that he wasn't interested in anything more than what we had. That should have convinced me. That should have been all that I needed to hear to make me walk away from him and chalk him up as a lesson learned. But, of course, it didn't. He was so incredibly manipulative. I can see that now. I know now that that is what it was, but I couldn't then. When I was there, when I was in it, all I felt was what I thought was love. I figured that it might just take him a little bit longer, but that if I felt this strongly, it had to be something more than just a casual attraction. I couldn't help myself. I had to keep pursuing him. I found out that he had been going to the Orion Corporation factory and I decided that I was going to follow him there. It would change up our routine, force him to hear me out while I explained why he should commit to me."

"What did you see there?"

Ilya's mind resisted her efforts to bring the memories forward. She didn't want to think about them. She didn't want to have to remember what it was like to live those last few moments of freedom in terror.

"I don't really know how to explain it. The building itself looked almost like it had already been abandoned. It was old and outdated from the outside. The parking lot was empty except for two cars and the pavement was broken up from all of the plants growing up through it. I recognized Ryan's car and went inside. I wanted to get a look of what was in there before I went, but the windows were boarded up or painted black, so I couldn't see anything."

"What happened when you went inside?"

"I don't even know how to describe the inside of the building. It was like the factory was in layers. Equipment that looked a century old or more was still there, but newer technology had been patched on top of it over and over to create these strange monster machines. The sound they made was ungodly. I couldn't even hear myself think. I went by the machinery so fast I didn't even see what it was doing."

"Did you see anything other than the machinery?"

"There were rooms," Ilya said. "I can only guess that they were the storage that the Valdicians were talking about. They were filled with crates marked 'Orion Corporation, Izalux'. Some of the other rooms were full of what looked like every part that they could possibly need to fix the machinery if it broke down, shipping supplies, and huge cases of what I assume was ingredients for the Izalux."

"Is that all?"

Ilya shook her head.

"I could hear something deep in the factory. It was voices, but I couldn't understand what they were saying. I followed them and saw more rooms and another floor of machines. Then I found a room that had been completely blacked out. The ceiling, floor, and windows were all totally black."

"Just like the women in the lab said the other day," Jonah pointed out.

Aubrey nodded.

"That room," she said. "Was there anything in it? Did you see anything other than the blackness?"

"I didn't really see it," Ilya said, "but it was like I could feel that there were people there looking at me. I knew that the room wasn't empty. I got away from it and went down the hallway as fast as I could. When I turned a corner, I saw another room that looked like the black one, but there was light coming out of it."

"Light?" Aubrey asked.

"Not a lot," Ilya said. "Not like there was a lamp turned on inside or there were bulbs in the ceiling or anything. Just a small amount of light. Faint. Almost silvery. I didn't want any of the people in there to see me, so I started back the way that I came. At least that's what I thought that I was doing. I ended up getting lost and in another wing of the factory. There was no machinery there, but I could hear more voices. These sounded scared, sometimes like they were crying. I couldn't open any of the doors that I found and there were no windows. The further that I went, the louder the voices got. Then I heard footsteps behind me."

"Why didn't you stop?" Jonah asked. "Why didn't you just find the nearest door out of the building and leave?"

Ilya turned toward him, her lips curved in a rueful smile.

"Because I knew that Ryan was somewhere in there," she said simply. "Nothing else really mattered to me then. I had to talk to him. I felt like I had no other choice. I knew that if I could just talk to him, if I could just tell him, then he would understand and we could be together."

"Tell him what?" Aubrey asked. "What was so important that you had to put yourself in danger like that just to talk to this guy?"

Ilya hesitated.

"I just needed to talk to him," she said firmly, hoping that the tone of her voice would tell them that she wasn't interested in going any further down that line of conversation.

"Did you ever find Ryan?" Jonah asked.

Ilya nodded.

"I did," she said. "I was so relieved. I knew that everything was going to be fine. We would talk and he would see that we were meant to be together. He would get me out of the factory and we would start our life together."

"What happened?" Gannon asked.

"It was all so fast," Ilya said. "One moment I was talking to Ryan and the next I was being dragged out of the room by these creatures in long robes. I had no idea what or who they were."

"Valdicians," Jonah said quietly.

Ilya nodded.

"They brought me into one of the rooms and that's all I remember from the factory. The next thing that I was aware of was being in the breeding facility in the lab. He had me hooked up to all kinds of machines and there were other women in the tanks around me. He never explained anything. I had to find out what was happening to me in the few minutes that I had to talk to the other women when we were doing our work."

"Work?" Aubrey asked.

"We spent a lot of our time in the tanks, but we also had to participate in other elements of the experiments. I think that Ryan got himself in over his head in a way. He had these tremendous visions for all of the amazing hybrids that he would be able to create and what he would be able to accomplish with them, but I don't think that he considered what it would take to sustain the powerful rapid growth that he achieved. The nursery and the training programs were handled by other hybrids or the men that Ryan chose, but the human women did things like cooking and sewing and cleaning unless our pregnancies showed signs of distress or we were undergoing tests. Interacting with the other women during those jobs was how I found out about everything that he was doing."

"If he had a personal relationship with you, though, at least he must have treated you better than the other women who were in the breeding program," Jonah said.

Ilya met his eyes again and let out a long breath.

"No," she said, shaking her head. "No."

13

———

"What is he doing here?"

Ellora tightened her grip around the spoon in her hand as she gestured toward Malcolm with it. Some of the bright red sauce that she was stirring splattered across the floor and the image made her shudder, but she didn't relent. Athan stepped forward, subtly putting himself between Ellora and Malcolm.

"Ellora," he said, holding out his hand as if trying to calm her and bring down the frantic energy that seemed to spark within her with the smallest catalyst since their time in the tunnels. "It's alright."

"What do you mean 'it's alright'?" she asked angrily. "What is that man doing in my kitchen?"

"He's here with us," Athan said, gesturing toward Rain and two of the humans from the settlement who had come along with them. "He's asked to join us."

Ellora blinked, feeling as though the words hadn't really made it all the way into her mind.

"Excuse me?" she asked.

She looked from Athan to Rain and then back to Athan.

"He's asked to join us," Athan said.

"He is a member of the Order," Ellora said, jabbing her spoon in Malcolm's direction. "He is working for them."

"He was," Athan relented. "He was sent to find Rain, me, and the rest of the humans that have agreed to come with us to Penthos. He was supposed to capture us and bring us back to stand before the Panel."

"And you trusted him?" Ellora asked in exasperation. "He was sent to ensure that you were killed and you brought him into my home? Into the headquarters of the war being fought partially against those he serves?"

"I want to defect," Malcolm said.

The younger man speaking for himself was a surprise and it struck Ellora silent. She looked at her brother, lowering the spoon only slightly as she waited for him to continue. When he remained silent, she gestured for him to keep going.

"Go on," she said.

Malcolm took a cautious step out from behind Athan and faced Ellora as if she were the only one who he cared about speaking to.

"I know that I have done things that were wrong and that I have been aligned with an organization that cannot be trusted, but assure you that I do not stand for what they do. I do not want to be a part of anything that they are doing. I'm sorry for all of the pain that I have caused or that I have contributed to, and I want to make amends. If you will permit me, I want to fight alongside you and do anything that I can to make things right."

Ellora looked back at Athan and shook her head.

"I can't make this decision," she said. "This isn't my choice to make. This situation is about all of us and we need to make decisions like this together. We need to get as many of the group together as possible and talk to them about this. I will go along with whatever decision that they make."

Athan nodded.

"I think that's reasonable. We'll gather in the meeting hall."

Ellora watched as the small group left her kitchen, Malcolm's eyes lingering on her as they walked away. There was a distant, painful look in them that made a hint of guilt flicker through her. She didn't intent to hurt or offend her brother, but she also couldn't let herself simply trust someone when they had already stood against her. There was too much at stake now, too much danger that they could be facing. When they had all left the house, Ellora turned back to the stove and finished the sauce. She touched the spoon to her tongue to sample it, enjoying the bright, sweet taste of the berries that seemed to burst on her tongue as she swallowed.

Pushing the pot to the back of the stove so that it could start to cool, she went to her bedroom to change clothes before leaving to head for the meeting hall. She didn't know how many of the group that Athan would be able to gather and she didn't want to miss any of the discussion. She had been completely honest when she said that she would go along with whatever decision the rest of the group made. Though she carried reservations and nervousness within herself, she knew that it wasn't just her thoughts and beliefs that mattered. Everyone who had agreed to be a part of this battle were willing to lay down their safety, their comfort, and even their lives to stand up for what they believed, and they deserved the respect of having their voices heard in as much of how it unfolded as possible.

The hall was already starting to fill up by the time that Ellora stepped in. Some were sitting close to the elevated platform on the far end while others milled around in small groups, their hushed voices occasionally rising high enough for her to hear that they were questioning why they were being called to the hall. Some worried that something had happened while others were concerned that the situation had reached a new peak and they were going to leave for Penthos without their training. Still others rejected both ideas, expressing excitement at the thought of starting their training and the skills that they would learn. The different conversations seemed to epitomize the emotions that Ellora was feeling.

Several minutes passed while she sat staring at the empty platform and then Athan, Malcolm, Rain, Rey, and Creia walked out onto it and faced the crowd. Athan lifted his hands up, gesturing for the group to sit. When the crowd had quieted, Athan briefly explained the situation. Ellora noticed that he didn't mention the Order or what that might mean. Instead, he said only that Malcolm had not been involved in the group thus far but had intelligence of some of their enemies. He told them that Malcolm had come to them against the wishes of those enemies to ask for their mercy and to offer his help. When he finished, Athan looked out over the group, taking the time to account for every person who was looking up at him. He stared into Ellora's eyes for a longer moment than the rest and she felt as though he were making a particular appeal to her. Though she had emphasized that they were a group and that they should do all things for the benefit and with the approval of the group, she knew that that was not the way that Athan saw it. She was Aegeus's wife and Maxim and Kyven's mother, which meant that she had precedence and importance over those who didn't have such strong affiliations. Her opinion was more valuable than the rest and it was her approval that he was seeking.

A few of the group stood and announced that they were loyal to the group and that whatever the leaders considered to be best for all of them they would willingly follow. They walked out of the hall to continue the preparations that they were making. Of the group that was left, one of the human men stood.

"I was there when Malcolm stopped us on our way back from the settlement," he said. "I watched his interaction with Rain, Athan, and Ellora. Though I couldn't hear what he said, I saw his face and the way that he acted. I believe that he is sincere in his desire to separate himself from his previous affiliations and assist us. I think that we should welcome him."

There were a few exclamations of agreement through the group and then a human woman stood up.

"I was there, too, and I know how terrified we were when we saw him. How are we to know that he is being honest? How do we know that what he's saying isn't just so that we'll trust him and he'll be able to learn our secrets? Wouldn't bringing him into our group and allowing him to be a part of our training be the most dangerous thing that we could do? We are facing enough of a risk. I don't think that we should make decisions that put us at even greater risk."

A few mutters through the group told Ellora that there were some who agreed with the woman's sentiments. The thought made her realize that when she sat quietly with the honest emotions that were within her she was being pulled toward trusting her brother, accepting him into their fold, and allowing him to prove himself. She kept quiet, wanting the give the group the freedom that she had promised. Felix, a Mikana man just a few months older than Maxim, stood.

"I wasn't there. I don't know what happened when Malcolm stopped you on the way here. I don't think that matters. What matters is what I'm seeing and hearing right now. This man is standing in front of us asking for our help. He has obviously gone through things that none of us know about, but it has been enough to convince him that he no longer wants to be a part of them. Malcolm knows the truth. He knows that our rebellion is what is right. I think that we should extend our trust to him."

"You're only saying that because he is one of your kind," another man from the settlement said.

The statement sent a scatter of gasps and bursts of anger throughout the rest of those in the meeting hall. Ellora jumped to her feet, no longer able to withhold her emotions.

"Don't start with that," Ellora said. "There is not a single one of us who is better than any other because of our species. Isn't that why we're here? Is there one of us who hasn't been threatened or looked down on purely because of who or what we are? Ryan has been breaking all of our kinds down bit by bit and creating hybrid creatures out of them to use as weapons. He doesn't see individuals when he looks at any of us. It doesn't matter whether we are Denynso, Mikana, human, Irisa, Eteri, or anything else. We are united in this and if there is any one of you who doesn't feel that way, then you need to leave and you need to leave now, but make no mistake. If you choose to leave, you will be counted among our enemies. We can trust someone who comes to us for help knowing what we stand for. We cannot trust someone who knows what we stand for and plan to do and then chooses to leave our ranks."

She looked to Athan and he gave a single nod, the shadow of a smile coming to his lips.

"I am asking all of you to look within yourself and remember what it is that is compelling you to fight. What drives you to stand up against our common enemy? All of you are making a decision that puts your life at risk and you are making it with a clear and determined heart. Now know that Malcolm is doing the same thing. Even more. I know that it is difficult to think of bringing someone who was once sworn against our cause into our fold and trusting him as you would trust any other, but I can tell you that what he says is true. Just the fact that he says that he wishes to leave his previous ranks and join ours is enough for me to know that he is fully committed. That statement alone would warrant a reaction that would be swift and severe. He wouldn't say it if it wasn't exactly what he meant and if he wasn't willing to fight for it."

Rey stepped forward and looked out over the room.

"I know that this situation is more than any of us ever expected to encounter. Even I don't know everything that is happening. But what I do know tells me that we need every person that we can get who is willing to stand beside us. Malcolm has come to us offering himself to our service. What we are fighting for is more than any single one of us, and far more impactful than our kinds, our homes, or our planet. There is not one among us who has not been misled at some time in our lives or who has not made a decision that we wish that we hadn't made. Malcolm is asking for redemption. I believe that I can speak both for myself and for Creia when I say that we will happily give it to him."

"So will I," Athan said.

"And me," Ellora said.

Gradually everyone in the room stood, offering their approval. Ellora felt her chest swell with emotion as she watched Malcolm fall to his knees again, his head hanging as if overwhelmed. Athan walked up to him and reached down to help him to his feet again, turning him so that the young man looked him directly in the face.

"You have been given asylum. You are now a part of us." He stepped back and reached behind his shoulder to wrap his hand around the handle of the sword strapped to his back. He withdrew it and laid it across his palms, holding it out to Malcolm. "Thank you for your sacrifice and for your devotion."

Malcolm reached out and took the sword into his hands.

"Thank you," he said. "I will serve you with all that I am."

"I know that you will."

Athan pulled Malcolm in for an embrace and Ellora could see the emotion on his face that told her he was happy and relieved that they had chosen to take Malcolm's offer and save him from the horror of the corrupt Order.

THE MEETING HALL was silent and empty, but Malcolm was still standing in the center of the platform, the sword that Athan had presented him rolling across his palm. He stared down at it with a greater sense of peace and confidence in him than he had had in as long as he could remember. Though the idea of turning his back on the Order and defecting to Athan's rebellion was terrifying, Malcolm also felt as though he had been freed, like a toxic breath within him had finally been released from his lungs, unclouding his mind, and putting him in control of himself again.

Athan had been resistant to allow him the time to himself that he requested, but he reassured him. It would take some time for the Order to truly know that he was now out of their reach and would not be bringing them Athan or any of the rest of the group. He had tonight. He would need the protection and perseverance of the rest for as long as they were on Uoria after, but he had tonight.

Malcolm was beginning to step down from the platform when he heard the door to the meeting hall open. His muscles tensed and his heart immediately started pounding, the beat erratic and strong in his temples. He adjusted his grip on the handle of the sword, priming himself to defend himself if attacked. It was possible that news of his abandonment of the Order and his vows of loyalty to them had spread to the Panel faster than he had thought that it would and they were now after him. If they knew that he was alone, they wouldn't hesitate to eliminate him.

The figure coming into the meeting hall stepped closer and he saw that it didn't seem to be large enough to be one of the men of the Order. Instead, it was small and moved fluidly, almost gliding across the floor as it came toward him. When it stepped into the light he saw that it was a delicate, beautiful woman. She gazed up at him with eyes a pale crystal blue that reminded him of the sky in the first moments after the pink of a sunrise faded away. Her thick hair was blond so pale it was nearly white and was tied behind her head in a series of braids. She glanced briefly over her shoulder and he saw that the braids met in the back to create a complex cage over the rest of her mane where it lay down to her waist. When she turned back to him her full lips held the faintest brush of a smile.

"Are you alright?" she asked.

It was almost as though Malcolm could feel her voice wash over him as she spoke. It was sweet and light, settling on his skin like a gentle mist of rain. He looked at his hands and realized that he was still holding the sword poised. He lowered it and drew it back so that it was slightly behind him.

"I'm sorry," he said. "I didn't know who you were."

"It's alright," she said, stepping up onto the platform with him. "I know who you are. Athan and Ellora asked that I host you in my home until you leave Uoria."

"They did?" Malcolm asked.

She nodded.

"They say that you no longer have somewhere safe to live."

Malcolm had the sudden, startling realization that they were right. He lived in a home with three other men, two of whom were also in the Order. He couldn't return there, leaving him with nowhere to live during the time that they spent on Uoria before leaving for Penthos.

"I don't want to impose on you," Malcolm said, not knowing any other option, but also not wanting to feel as though he were causing this beautiful woman any difficulty.

"You won't be imposing," she said. "I wouldn't have accepted if I didn't want you there. You are incredibly brave, Malcolm. I know the danger that you are facing with the decision that you have made, and I am honored to give you any help that I can."

"Thank you. What is your name?"

"Icelyn," she said, offering her hand in the traditional Mikana greeting.

"Malcolm," he said, his skin tingling as his hand touched hers.

Icelyn smiled wider, the expression getting into her eyes and causing them to sparkle.

"I know," she said.

She turned, giving Malcolm a glance over her shoulder before stepping down off of the platform and starting toward the door to the meeting hall. He winced, embarrassed by introducing himself to her only moments after she said his name, but followed her eagerly. There was a flicker of nervousness in his belly when they reached the door as he worried that the Order would be waiting for them, but when they stepped outside he found the courtyard empty. They walked along in silence for a few moments before Icelyn turned to him again.

"I hope that you won't be disappointed by my house," she said. "It's not much, but I'm comfortable there."

"I'm sure that it will be everything that I could need," he said.

Her lovely eyes slid to him, but she didn't say anything more. They continued on toward one of the clusters of homes and Malcolm looked around the village with greater appreciation. It felt like for so long he had been seeing his surroundings only through the prism of the Order, unable to take in the details that were always there and yet seemed to have only just appeared again.

They arrived at a small home and Icelyn opened the door. She stepped inside and pressed her hand to the wall to trigger the glowing lights embedded near the top of the walls.

"Come in," she said.

Malcolm stepped into the house and looked around the modest but inviting room. It was very much like the house that he had been living in, but smaller, designed for one person or a couple rather than several single men as his house was. The furniture was sparse but looked comfortable and the delicate decorative touches added just the hint of feminine detail, softening the impact of the entire space. The room where they were standing served as the living area on one half and the kitchen on the other, and he could see a short hallway leading further into the home where he assumed there would be a bedroom and bathroom. He had no belongings with him and didn't want to make any presumptions about the space, so he remained still.

"I really appreciate you doing this," he said as Icelyn walked into the kitchen and took a canister of coffee from a shelf.

She started the machine on the counter and picked up two mugs, placing them within the machine to fill before handing one to him.

"Welcome home."

14

TO BE CONTINUED...

Creia settled onto the pallet of blankets and pillows that Theia had made on the floor beside the bed that was too small to accommodate them. Though it had been a few weeks since their arrival in the Mikana kingdom, he still felt as though he was getting accustomed to being outside of his compound and in surroundings that were not familiar and not designed for his kind. He was used to being in the compound, the only King influencing those around him, but now he was learning to balance his cooperation with the other species that had gathered in the kingdom while also planning for the battles that lay ahead.

Theia slipped into place beside him and rested her head on her mate's shoulder. He drew in a breath of her, comforted by the presence of her close to him. It had been so long since they had completed their bond that he could hardly remember a time before her. She was as irremovably connected to him as he was to her and he knew in his heart that he wouldn't be complete if he had to spend even a moment without her as his mate.

"Do you think that we are adequately prepared for the war?" he asked.

Theia lifted her head slightly as if to look at him, but Creia couldn't see her in the dark of the room.

"What do you mean?" she asked.

"I don't know if the people we have to bring with us to Penthos are going to be enough. We don't know the size of the hybrid army or what they are capable of doing."

"You have been so confident," Theia said. "You said that there was nothing that was going to keep us from victory."

"I know, and I believe that we are the most powerful of any army that could confront Ryan and his hybrids, but is it enough? Do we have enough people to be fully confident when we step onto that planet that we are going to be able to face them down and come out triumphant?"

"I don't know," Theia admitted. "I will ensure that those we have are trained as well as possible and that they are as prepared as they can be to fight in whatever ways the hybrid army uses. They will need to see that you believe in them, that you are not concerned about their efforts or their abilities. You must be strong for them, Creia."

"I know," he said. "But I have seen what the Valdicians are capable of doing. I've seen the severity of what they can do. They are only the minions of Ryan. They are only the servants of the man who has created the army that we are preparing to fight. If they are capable of the ferocity that I witnessed when they held me captive, what is Ryan capable of? What has he trained his army to do?"

"What do you think we should do?" Theia asked. "We have already gathered all of those from the compound, the Mikana kingdom, and the Nyx 23 settlement who are willing to come with us. Who else could we ask?"

"Perhaps we should reach out to the Eteri," Creia said.

"Some already have," Theia said. "They brought Azrael and Ariella with them to Earth."

"I know. But that's it. There are only two of their kind on Penthos right now and only one of them is a warrior. They are among the strongest and most skilled warriors outside of the Denynso that I have ever encountered. They have capabilities that are far beyond anything that our kind has. Even Loralia is only able to utilize some of the skills of the kind and that is half of her blood. I am certain that Ryan has used Eteri blood to create some of his hybrids so that his weapons would be able to access those skills. We need warriors who will be able to counter those hybrids. This is a war unlike anything that we have ever encountered. We can't just use the same strategies that we always have and expect that we will get the same results. We need levels of attack, layers of strategy that will allow us to match each of the hybrids, skill for skill, drive for drive. If we can't, we must be able to overcome them. I need to go talk to the Eteri."

Theia rested her head on his shoulder again and nodded.

"We can leave in the morning," she said. "I'm sure that Kyven, Rey, and the Mikana army can handle the beginning of the training until we return."

"No," Creia said. "You must stay here. This is something that I need to do alone. Besides, they need you here. They need your guidance. I will get there and back as fast as I can."

"Are you sure that you'll be safe alone?" Theia asked. "Won't the Order be looking for you?"

"They might," Creia said, "but there's nothing that I can do to stop that. We need the Eteri. It has been a long time since the Denynso have called upon them, but the time's come. I need to ask for their help. It can only come from me."

THE NEXT MORNING, Creia boarded one of the vehicles that Athan had stolen for their use and started across the planet. He traveled as quickly as he could, pausing only when exhaustion made it absolutely necessary for him to pause. When he did, it was for the shortest time possible before he continued on. He followed the most direct route, though he knew that it would put him at the highest risk. Choosing to swerve as he went or to take different directions that deviated from the straight route could have distracted anyone who might be following him, but it also would have taken him off course and wasted precious time that he simply couldn't afford to lose. Whatever risk that it posed him, he had to move across the planet as fast as he possibly could. Those in the Mikana kingdom needed their training and those on Penthos couldn't be kept waiting for any longer than was absolutely unavoidable.

Creia didn't know how long he had been traveling when he finally saw that he was approaching the compound. He had been away from his home for longer than he had ever been and he felt himself drawn to it, as if magnetized by the comfort and familiarity of it. He wanted to go back into the compound, to walk back through the banquet hall and sit on his throne, to climb the stairs and rest in his own bed. The more that he longed for the compound, however, the harder that he pushed himself away from it. He couldn't go back there. Not now. Not yet. There was so much more that he needed to accomplish. As he moved past the compound Creia had to remind himself that the clan wasn't there, that with the exception of the few women born into the families and the aged, the vast majority of the Denynso had reported to the Mikana kingdom to serve. He had left only Verity in his place, knowing that the years that the woman had lived and all that she had seen in her time as a midwife and the nurturer of the clan before Ty came of age would make her a strong and wise interim leader. She would protect his home until he was able to return and ensure that when they returned victorious, the compound would be prepared to welcome them.

He knew that it was his final night before he arrived at the Eteri village and Creia brought the vehicle to a stop, wanting to rest and refresh himself so that he would be prepared to go before the Eteri leader. Just as he had every other time that he stopped on his journey across Uoria, Creia stopped where he could conceal the vehicle and make as little change in the surroundings with his presence as possible so that he could guard himself from any who might be pursuing him. Though he hadn't encountered the Order during his travel, that came as no comfort, no reassurance to him. Rather than making him feel that he might be safe and that they weren't coming after him, it only increased his tension and anxiety, making him feel as though were only getting closer to the danger with each passing moment.

Once the vehicle was as hidden as he could make it, Creia walked across the rocky shore of the pond on the very edge of the Denynso compound. Though he knew that he couldn't go to the village or do anything that might tell those of the clan who had stayed behind that he was there, he hadn't been able to resist just this small part of the compound. He felt centered being within the parameters of the compound, even though he was still distanced from the stone wall that defined the primary area. This was a place that was sacred to him, a place where he had spent a considerable amount of time and that held many memories for him. Just standing on the bank and looking out over the purple water of the pond brought peace to his heart and allowed his mind to quiet.

Kneeling at the edge of the water, Creia dipped his hands in and filled his palms. The color of the water was so rich when it was within the deep pond that it looked almost black, but now that it was just a shallow pool against his skin the color was clearer and more vibrant. The thickly mineral smell of the water felt nearly as fortifying as food and pouring the handful down over his head seemed to purify and cleanse him. Creia closed his eyes and tilted his head back toward the skin. He could feel the drops of water sliding down his face and dripping onto his chest. When the calm had fully surrounded him, Creia opened his eyes and looked back into the water. Pebbles shimmered just beneath the surface at the very edge of the pond where the water lapped up against the bank and he reached in to scoop them up. He brought two handfuls of the pebbles back across the bank toward the camp that he had set up for himself. Spreading them out across the ground in front of his tent to dry, he climbed inside the meager shelter and wrapped himself tightly in the thick, warm blanket that still smelled of Theia and let himself fall deeply to sleep.

THE ETERI VILLAGE looked so much the same as Creia remembered it, yet the differences were distinct, reminding him of the time that had passed since he had been welcomed within the borders of the lush, beautiful area of the planet. He could hear the rush of the wind through the ferns and low-hanging branches of the fruit trees and smell the swiftly moving water and bright floral blooms. It was still early, but within a few moments of him approaching the village, he heard a new sound, a fluttering that told him that one of the Eteri was nearby.

Creia paused and looked around, knowing all too well that this species could be shy and fleeting, difficult to get close to, especially for those that the Eteri didn't know or trust. He took a few slow, cautious steps forward toward the thick forest and peered into the shadows. Finally, he saw the glimmer of faintly colored light cut through the darkness in a quick flicker.

"Hello?" he called toward the light.

The flicker appeared again and he remained still, not wanting to startle whoever it was that was in the trees watching him. A moment later he saw another flicker, this one a shade of green that nearly blended in with the leaves around it.

"I mean you no harm," he said.

A few seconds later a slender figure stepped around one of the trees to face him. It was a lovely woman, the glow around her timid, but the expression in her eyes curious. She stared at Creia, her head tilting to one side and then the other.

"Who are you?" she asked.

There was no aggression in the question, no anger or fear. There was only soft, musical curiosity.

"My name is Creia," he said. "I am King of the Denynso compound that is just..."

"I know where it is," the woman said. "Why have you come here? Did the rest send you?"

"The rest?" Creia asked.

"Those who were already here," she explained. "I met some of your kind. They were younger than you."

Creia nodded.

"The warriors are all younger than me," he said. "Many of them are my children."

The woman shook her head.

"Not in years," she said. "In their hearts. You are carrying so much in yours. Too many years. Too much."

The words crashed into Creia's chest and he felt like he needed to draw in a harder breath just so that he was able to normalize himself.

"I need to speak with your King."

The woman laughed and shook her head.

"No," she said.

"No?" Creia asked, startled by her abrupt rejection of his request. "I am not permitted to speak to the King?"

The woman shook her head.

"No," she said.

Creia felt himself becoming defensive.

"Why not?" he asked.

"We don't have one," the woman replied. "We have a Queen."

It was said with sincerity, not as though she wanted to frustrate or anger him, but as if it genuinely amused her that he would wish to speak to a King when they may not have had such a ruler in a generation or more.

"May I speak to her?" Creia asked. "It is extremely important."

"Of course," she said. "Come with me."

They made their way through the forest and toward the palace. It was just as he remembered it. Unlike the royal homes of many other species, the palace of the Eteri wasn't massively large or imposing. In fact, it showed little difference from the other homes around it. The only clear differentiation was the position, lifted up slightly higher than the rest to afford the Queen inside a clearer view of all of her kind. The woman who guided him stepped up to the door to the palace and knocked on it softly. A few seconds later, it opened.

"Good morning, Evangeline," the woman who opened the door said. "What can I do for you?"

Evangeline gestured toward Creia.

"I found him on the far edge of the forest," she said. "He didn't come through the tunnels. He says that he needs to talk to you about something extremely important."

The Queen looked at Creia and he could see her eyes scrutinizing him, trying to understand why he might be there.

"You are Denynso," she said, not a question but a statement.

"Yes," Creia said.

"If you didn't travel through the tunnels, that means that you know how to access the village through the ancient means."

"Yes."

"That can only mean..."

"He is King," Evangeline said.

The woman straightened and drew in a breath.

"Is this true?" she asked.

Creia nodded.

"Yes," he said. "But I come unarmed and alone. I wish to speak to you about a situation of the gravest importance."

"I am Elsavetta, Queen of the Eteri. You once knew my grandfather."

Recognition washed over him and Creia was struck by a memory of this woman when she was just a child playing at the feet of her grandfather when he was King.

"I remember," he said. "Meirion was a good man."

"He still is," Elsavetta said. "He simply is no longer King."

Creia nodded again and waited until the Queen stepped back into her palace, clearing a space for him to step inside with her.

"Please, come in." She glanced at the young Eteri would had escorted Creia to the palace. "Thank you, Evangeline."

Evangeline smiled and walked away, soon sinking back into the cover of the trees and joining the faint green glow of the Eteri who had remained concealed even as they traveled through the forest.

"Are you hungry?" Elsavetta asked. "We can discuss what has brought you here over breakfast."

Creia had stopped so little when he was traveling that he had barely eaten and now he felt the hunger gnawing at his stomach. He nodded.

"Yes. Thank you."

He followed Elsavetta into a small room off of the main chamber of the palace and settled onto a low couch that barely accommodated his body. A few moments later another winged woman came into the room carrying a tray of food. She settled it onto a table in between them and handed Creia and Elsavetta each a small cup of a beverage that smelled strongly of the fruit and flowers from the forest. He took a sip and then set the cup down, far more interested in the elaborate pastries on the tray. He waited until Elsavetta had chosen one and then reached for the one closest to him. The flavor was rich and unexpected, the savory filling a bold and delectable contrast to the sweet outside. The Queen gave him a few moments to eat before speaking again.

"So, what brings you here, Creia?"

The King finished the pastry in his hand and took

another sip of the tea. Feeling bolstered by the food, he started to tell her about what was happening. He knew that she would know of the Order and what they were capable of doing. Her kind had already witnessed the wrath of the corrupt members and had marched into battle alongside Aegeus. Several had been with him the day that he died. When he was finished, Creia sat back and stared at Elsavetta, waiting for her response.

"It has been many years since you have had any contact with the Eteri," she said. "I have not even seen you since I was a small child and my grandfather never spoke of you again after the final time that I saw you. I don't know what happened between you, but I know that it changed so much. It has been many, many years since the Eteri and the Denynso have enjoyed an alliance."

"But that alliance was powerful," Creia said. "Our kinds enjoyed a closer alliance than either of us have maintained with any other species."

"That was not the first time that the alliance ended, however," Elsavetta said. "Many generations ago our kinds were closely linked but then fell away from each other. Then we drew close again only to have you turn your back on us."

"That was not my intention," Creia said. "I never meant to turn my back on the Eteri. I admit that it was the fears and the hesitations of the Denynso that closed off our cooperation." He paused and took a breath, touching his hand to his chest to show his sincerity. "It was my fears and hesitations. I know that the Denynso have been isolated. There are many of my kind that never even knew of the Eteri until recently. I apologize for that. I know that we have not been there for you in the way that we should have been and that there is little that I can say that will show you my sincerity and earn your trust, but I ask that you put that faith in us. I know that two of your kind have already joined us and are currently on the battlefield. They are making a powerful difference, but we need more. We need as much strength and force as we can bring."

Elsavetta hesitated and Creia felt his heart pounding in his chest, regret for the years that he had kept his kind blocked off from the rest of the planet blending with fear to create a sharp bitterness that flowed through his blood.

"Creia," the Queen started, but he didn't give her a chance to continue.

"Please," he said. "I'm not here to represent my kind. I am not here as King. I am not here to symbolize the Denynso reaching out to the Eteri. This is just me. I am here personally asking for your help."

"Why now?" Elsavetta asked. "You made it clear that you had your reasons for separating the Denynso from the Eteri, just as the King did so many generations ago. What is changing it now so that you would humble yourself before me? Why would you think that striving to repair the relationship between the Denynso and the Eteri would make a difference now?"

Creia met her eyes.

"The war is rising. Alliances that were broken for the protection of Uoria must now be resumed for the protection of all of existence."

www.ingramcontent.com/pod-product-compliance
Lightning Source LLC
Chambersburg PA
CBHW032028180726
48284CB00008B/2523